D0123046

the TERRIBLE THING that happened to BARNABY BROCKET

Also by John Boyne

The Boy in the Striped Pajamas
Noah Barleywater Runs Away

the TERRIBLE THING that happened to BARNABY BROCKET

JOHN BOYNE

illustrated by
OLIVER JEFFERS

ALFRED A. KNOPF
NEW YORK

THIS IS A BORZOI BOOK PUBLISHED BY ALFRED A. KNOPF

This is a work of fiction. Names, characters, places, and incidents either are the product of the author's imagination or are used fictitiously. Any resemblance to actual persons, living or dead, events, or locales is entirely coincidental.

 Published in the United States by Alfred A. Knopf, an imprint of Random House Children's Books, a division of Random House, Inc., New York. Originally published in the United Kingdom by Random House Group Ltd., London, in 2012.

Library of Congress Cataloging-in-Publication Data is available upon request.

ISBN 978-0-307-97762-5 (hc) — ISBN 978-0-307-97763-2 (lib. bdg.) —
ISBN 978-0-307-97764-9 (ebook)

The text of this book is set in 12-point ITC New Baskerville.

Printed in the United States of America

January 2013
10 9 8 7 6 5 4 3 2 1

First U.S. Edition

For Philip Ardagh
—John Boyne

the TERRIBLE THING that happened to BARNABY BROCKET

Chapter 1

A Perfectly Normal Family

This is the story of Barnaby Brocket, and to understand Barnaby, first you have to understand his parents: two people who were so afraid of anyone who was different that they did a terrible thing that would have the most appalling consequences for everyone they loved.

We begin with Barnaby's father, Alistair, who considered himself to be a completely normal man. He led a normal life in a normal house, lived in a normal neighborhood where he did normal things in a normal way. His wife was normal, as were his two children.

Alistair had no time for people who were unusual or who made a show of themselves in public. When he was sitting on a Metro train and a group of teenagers were talking loudly nearby, he would wait until the next stop, jump off, and move to a different carriage before the doors could close again. When he was eating in a restaurant—not one of those fancy new restaurants with difficult menus and confusing food; a normal one—he grew irritated if his evening was spoiled by waiters singing "Happy Birthday" to some attention-seeking diner.

He worked as a solicitor at the firm of Bother & Blastit in the most magnificent city in the world—Sydney, Australia—where he specialized in last wills and testaments, a rather grim employment that suited him down to the ground. It was a perfectly normal thing, after all, to prepare a will. Nothing unusual in that. When clients came to see him in his office, they often found themselves a little nervous, for drawing up a will can be a difficult or distressing matter.

"Please don't upset yourself," Alistair would say on such occasions. "It's perfectly normal to die. We all have to do it one day. Imagine how awful it would be if we lived forever! The planet would collapse under all that excess weight."

Which is not to say that Alistair cared very much about the planet's welfare; he didn't. Only hippies and New Age types worried about things like that.

There is a belief held by some, particularly by those who live in the Far East, that each of us—you included—comprises one half of a couple separated before birth in the vast and complex universe, and that we spend our lives searching for that detached soul who can make us feel whole again. Until that day comes, we all feel a little out of sorts. Sometimes completeness is found through meeting someone who, on first appearances, seems to be the opposite of who we are. A man who likes art and poetry, for example, might end up falling in love with a woman who spends her afternoons up to her elbows in engine grease. A healthy-eating lady with an interest in outdoor sports might find herself drawn to a fellow who enjoys nothing more than watching them from the comfort of his living-room armchair with a beer in one hand and a sandwich in the other. It takes all sorts, after all. But Alistair Brocket always knew that he could never share his life with someone who wasn't as normal as he was, even though that in itself would have been a perfectly normal thing to do.

Which brings us to Barnaby's mother, Eleanor.

Eleanor Bullingham grew up on Beacon Hill, in a small house overlooking the northern beaches of Sydney. She had always been the apple of her parents' eyes, for she was indisputably the best-behaved girl in the neighborhood. She never crossed the street until the crossing guard appeared, even if there wasn't a car anywhere in sight. She stood up to let elderly people take her seat on the bus, even if there were dozens of empty seats already available to them. In fact, she was such a well-mannered little girl that when her grandmother

Elspeth died, leaving her a collection of one hundred vintage handkerchiefs with her initials, *EB,* carefully embroidered onto each one, she resolved one day to marry a man whose surname also began with *B* in order that her inheritance would not go to waste.

Like Alistair, she became a solicitor, specializing in property work, which, as she told anyone who asked her, she found frightfully interesting.

She accepted a job at Bother & Blastit almost a year after her future husband, and was a little disappointed at first when she looked around the office to discover how many of the young men and women employed there were behaving in a less-than-professional manner.

Very few of them kept their desks in any sort of tidy condition. Instead, they were covered with photographs of family members, pets, or, worse, celebrities. The men tore their used takeaway coffee cups into shreds as they talked loudly on the telephone, creating an unsightly mess for others to clean up later, while the women appeared to do nothing but eat all day, buying small snacks from a trolley that reappeared every few hours laden down with sweet treats in brightly colored packaging. Yes, this was normal behavior by the current standards of what was normal, but still, it wasn't *normal* normal.

At the beginning of her second week at the firm,

she found herself walking up two flights of stairs to a different department in order to deliver a hugely important document to a colleague who needed it without a moment's delay or the whole world would grind to a halt. Opening the door, she tried not to stare at the signs of disorder and squalor that lay before her in case it made her regurgitate her breakfast. But then, to her surprise, she saw something—or someone—who made her heart give the most unexpected little leap, like an infant gazelle hurdling triumphantly across a stream for the first time.

Sitting at a corner desk, with a neat pile of paperwork before him separated into color-coded groups, was a rather dashing young man, dressed in a pinstripe suit and sporting neatly parted hair. Unlike the barely house-trained animals who were working around him, he kept his desk tidy, the pens and pencils gathered together in a simple storage container, his documents laid out efficiently before him as he worked on them. There wasn't a picture of a child, a dog, or a celebrity anywhere in sight.

"That young man," she asked a girl sitting at the desk closest to her, stuffing her face with a banana nut muffin, the crumbs falling across her computer keyboard and getting lost forever between the keys. "The one sitting in the corner. What's his name?"

"You mean Alistair?" said the girl, running her teeth along the inside of the wrapper just in case there was any sticky toffee sauce left behind. "The most boring man in the universe?"

"What's his surname?" asked Eleanor hopefully.

"Brocket. Rotten, isn't it?"

"It's perfect," said Eleanor.

And so they were married. It was the normal thing to do, particularly after they had been to the theater together (three times); a local ice cream parlor (twice); a dance hall (only once; they hadn't liked it very much—far too much jiving going on, too much of that nasty rock-and-roll music); and on a day trip to Luna Park, where they took photographs and made pleasant conversation until the sun began to descend and the lights gleaming from the clown's giant face made him look even more terrifying than usual.

Exactly a year after their happy day, Alistair and Eleanor, now living in a normal house in Kirribilli on the Lower North Shore, welcomed their first child, Henry, into the world. He was born on a Monday morning on the stroke of nine o'clock, weighed precisely seven pounds, and appeared after only a short labor, smiling politely at the doctor who delivered him. Eleanor didn't cry or scream when she was giving birth, unlike some of those vulgar mothers whose antics polluted the television airwaves every night; in fact, the birth was an extremely polite affair, ordered and well mannered, and nobody took any offense at all.

Like his parents, Henry was a very well-behaved little boy, taking his bottle when it was offered to him, eating his food, looking absolutely mortified whenever he soiled his nappy. He grew at a normal rate, learning to speak by the time he turned two and understanding the letters of the alphabet a year later. When he was four, his kindergarten teacher told Alistair and Eleanor that she had nothing good or bad to report about their son, that he was perfectly normal in every way, and as a reward they bought him an ice cream on the way home that afternoon. Vanilla-flavored, of course.

Their second child, Melanie, was born on a Tuesday three years later. Like her brother, she presented no problems to either nurses or teachers, and by the time her fourth birthday had arrived, when her parents were already looking forward to the arrival of another baby, she was spending most of her time reading or playing with dolls in her bedroom, doing nothing that might mark her out as different from any of the other children who lived on their street.

There was really no doubt: the Brocket family was just about the most normal family in New South Wales, if not the whole of Australia.

And then their third child was born.

Barnaby Brocket emerged into the world on

a Friday, at twelve o'clock at night, which was already a bad start, as Eleanor was concerned that she might be keeping the doctor and nurse from their beds.

"I do apologize for this," she said, perspiring badly, which was embarrassing. She had never perspired at all when giving birth to Henry or Melanie; she had simply emitted a gentle glow, like the dying moments of a forty-watt bulb.

"It's quite all right, Mrs. Brocket," said Dr. Snow. "Children will appear when they appear. We have no way of controlling these things."

"Still, it is rather rude," said Eleanor before letting loose a tremendous scream as Barnaby decided that his moment was upon him. "Oh dear," she added, her face flushed from all these exertions.

"There's really nothing to worry about," insisted the doctor, getting himself into position to catch the slippery infant—rather like a rugby player stepping back on the field of play, one foot rooted firmly in the grass behind him, the other pressed forward in the soil, his two hands outstretched as he waits for the prize to be thrown in his direction.

Eleanor screamed again, then lay back, gasping in surprise. She felt a tremendous pressure building inside her body and wasn't sure how much longer she could stand it.

"Push, Mrs. Brocket!" said Dr. Snow, and Eleanor

screamed for a third time as she forced herself to push as hard as she could while the nurse placed a cold compress on her forehead. But rather than finding this a comfort, she began to wail loudly and then uttered a word she had never uttered in her life, a word that she found extremely offensive whenever anyone at Bother & Blastit employed it. It was a short word. One syllable. But it seemed to express everything she was feeling at that particular moment.

"That's the stuff," cried Dr. Snow cheerfully. "Here he comes now! One, two, three, and then a final giant push, all right? One . . ."

Eleanor breathed in.

"Two . . ."

She gasped.

"Three!"

And now there was a terrific sensation of relief and the sound of a baby crying. Eleanor collapsed back on the bed and groaned, glad that this horrible torture was over at last.

"Oh dear me," said Dr. Snow a moment later, and Eleanor lifted her head off the pillow in surprise.

"What's wrong?" she asked.

"It's the most extraordinary thing," he said as Eleanor sat up, despite the pain she was in, to get a better look at the baby who was provoking such an abnormal response.

the birth of BARNABY

"But where is he?" she asked, for he wasn't being cradled in Dr. Snow's hands, nor was he lying at the end of the bed. And that was when she noticed that both doctor and nurse were not looking at her anymore, but were staring with open mouths up toward the ceiling, where a newborn baby—*her* newborn baby—was pressed flat against the white rectangular tiles, looking down at the three of them with a cheeky smile on his face.

"He's up there," said Dr. Snow in amazement, and it was true: he was. For Barnaby Brocket, the third child of the most normal family who had ever lived in the Southern Hemisphere, was already proving himself to be anything but normal by refusing to obey the most fundamental rule of all.

The law of gravity.

Chapter 2

The Mattress on the Ceiling

Barnaby was discharged from hospital three days later and brought home to meet Henry and Melanie for the first time.

"Your brother's a little different from the rest of us," Alistair told them over breakfast that morning, choosing his words carefully. "I'm sure it's only a temporary thing but it's very upsetting. Just don't stare at him, all right? If he thinks he's getting a reaction, it will only encourage his foolishness."

The children looked at each other in surprise, unsure what their father could possibly mean by this.

"Does he have two heads?" asked Henry, reaching for the marmalade. He liked a bit of marmalade on his toast in the mornings. Although not in the evenings; then, he preferred strawberry jam.

"No, of course he doesn't have two heads,"

replied Alistair irritably. "Who on earth has two heads?"

"A two-headed sea monster," said Henry, who had recently been reading a book about a two-headed sea monster named Orco, which had caused any amount of mayhem beneath the Indian Ocean.

"I can assure you that your brother is not a two-headed sea monster," said Alistair.

"Does he have a tail?" asked Melanie, gathering up the empty bowls and stacking them neatly in the dishwasher. The family dog, Captain W. E. Johns, a canine of indeterminate breed and parentage, looked up at the word *tail* and began to chase his own around the kitchen, spinning in a circular direction until he fell over and lay on the floor, panting happily, delighted with himself.

"Why would a baby boy have a tail?" asked Alistair, sighing deeply. "Really, children, you have the most extraordinary imaginations. I don't know where you get them from. Neither your mother nor I have any imagination at all, and we certainly didn't bring you up to have one."

"I'd like to have a tail," said Henry thoughtfully.

"I'd like to be a two-headed sea monster," said Melanie.

"Well, you don't," snapped Alistair, glaring at his son. "And you aren't," he added, pointing at his daughter. "So let's just get back to being normal human beings and make sure this place is spick-and-span, all right? We have a guest coming this morning, remember."

"But he's not a guest, surely," said Henry, frowning. "He's our little brother."

"Yes, of course," said Alistair after only the briefest of pauses.

It was a little over an hour later when Eleanor pulled up outside in a taxi, holding a restless Barnaby in her arms.

"You've got a lively one there," said the driver as he turned the engine off, but Eleanor ignored the remark, as she disliked getting into conversations with strangers, particularly those who worked in the service industry. Her handbag fell into the gap between the two front seats, and as she reached for it, she let go of the baby for a moment and he floated off her knees, drifted upward, and bumped his head on the ceiling.

"Ow," gurgled Barnaby Brocket.

"You want to keep ahold of that lad," remarked the taxi driver, staring at him with world-weary eyes. "He'll get away from you if you're not careful."

"Thirty dollars, was it?" asked Eleanor, handing across a twenty and a ten as she realized that, yes, he might. If she wasn't careful.

As she entered the house, the children ran to

greet their mother, almost knocking her over in their excitement.

"But he's so small," said Henry in surprise. (In this regard at least, Barnaby was perfectly normal.)

"He smells delicious," said Melanie, giving him a good sniff. "Like a mixture of ice cream and maple syrup. What's his name anyway?"

"Can we call him Jim Hawkins?" asked Henry, who had taken to classic adventure stories in a big way.

"Or Peter the Goatherd?" asked Melanie, who always followed where her elder brother led.

"His name is Barnaby," said Alistair, coming over now and placing a kiss on his wife's cheek. "After your grandfather. And your grandfather's grandfather."

"Can I hold him?" asked Melanie, reaching forward, her arms outstretched.

"Not just now," said Eleanor.

"Can *I* hold him?" asked Henry, whose arms reached farther than his sister's, as he was three years older.

"No one is holding Barnaby," snapped Eleanor. "No one except your father or me. For the time being anyway."

"I'd rather not hold him just now, if it's all the same to you," said Alistair, staring at his son as if he was something that had escaped from a zoo and should be sent back there before he caused any damage to the soft furnishings.

"Well, he's your responsibility too," snapped Eleanor. "Don't think I'm taking care of this . . . this . . ."

"Baby?" suggested Melanie.

"Yes, I suppose that's as good a word as any. Don't think I'm taking care of this baby all on my own, Alistair."

"I'm happy to help, of course," said Alistair, looking away. "But you *are* his mother."

"And you're his father!"

"He seems to have bonded with you, though. Look at him."

Alistair and Eleanor looked down at Barnaby's face and he smiled up at them, kicking his arms and legs in delight, but neither parent smiled back. Henry and Melanie looked at each other in surprise. They weren't used to their parents speaking in such a brusque fashion. They fished out the present they'd bought the previous day by pooling their pocket money.

"It's for Barnaby," said Melanie, handing it across. "To welcome him into the family." In her hands she held a small gift-wrapped box, and Eleanor felt her heart soften a little at the welcome they were showing their little brother. She reached out to take the gift, but the moment she did so, Barnaby began to float upward once again, his blanket slipping away from him and falling to the floor as he drifted toward the ceiling, which was a much farther distance to travel than the roof of the taxi cab. It was also much harder on his head.

"Ow," grunted Barnaby Brocket, his tiny body stretched out flat as he looked down at his family, a decidedly grumpy expression on his face now.

"Oh, Alistair!" cried Eleanor, throwing up her arms in despair. Henry and Melanie said nothing; they simply stared up with their mouths wide open and expressions of wonder on their faces.

Captain W. E. Johns appeared, yawning, roused from sleep, and looked at the family that kept him fed, watered, and imprisoned before following the direction of the children's gaze until he too saw Barnaby on the ceiling, at which point his tail began to wag fiercely and he started to bark.

"Bark!" he barked. "Bark! Bark! Bark!"

A little later—although not quite as soon as you might expect—Alistair climbed on a chair to retrieve his son, taking charge of him now, as Eleanor had retired to bed with a mug of hot milk and a headache. Reluctantly, he gave Barnaby his bottle, then changed his nappy, placing a new one under the baby's bottom just as Barnaby decided to go again, in a perfect golden arc in the air. Finally, Alistair placed him in his basket, clipping the straps from Henry's rucksack across the top so he couldn't float up. At last Barnaby went to sleep and probably dreamed of something funny.

"Melanie, keep an eye on your brother," said Alistair, positioning his daughter in the seat next to him. "Henry, come with me, please."

Father and son crossed the garden to their neighbor's house and knocked on the front door.

"What do you need, Brocket?" asked grumpy old Mr. Cody, picking a flake of tobacco from between his front teeth and flicking it to the ground at their feet.

"The loan of your van," explained Alistair. "And its accompanying trailer. Just for an hour or two, that's all. And of course I'll compensate you for the gas."

Permission granted, Alistair and Henry drove across the Harbour Bridge into the city and made their way to a large department store on Market Street, where they purchased three large mattresses, each of which was designed for a double bed, a box of twelve-inch nails, and a hammer. Returning home, they dragged the mattresses into the living room, where Melanie was sitting exactly where they'd left her, staring at her sleeping baby brother.

"How was he?" asked Alistair. "Any problems?"

"No," said Melanie, shaking her head. "He's been asleep the whole time."

"Good. Well, take him into the kitchen, there's a good girl. I have a job to do in here."

He took two ladders from the garden shed and placed them at either end of the living room, then climbed one, holding the left-hand side of a mattress as he did so, while Henry climbed the other, holding the right.

"Hold it steady now," said Alistair as he took the first long nail from his breast pocket and used the hammer to pin the corner of the mattress to the ceiling. The nail went through easily enough but met a bit of resistance in the floorboards of the upstairs room. Still, it didn't take too long until he got it right.

"Now the other corner," he said, moving his ladder across and nailing the next part of the mattress in place. He continued doing this for almost an hour, using twenty-four nails in total, and by the time he finished, the previously white ceiling had been covered over by the rather flowery design of a David Jones Bellissimo plush medium mattress.

"What do you think?" asked Alistair, looking down at his son for approval.

"It's unusual," replied Henry, considering it.

"I'll give you that," agreed Alistair.

By now, the sound of all that hammering had woken Barnaby and he was making a series of unintelligible gurgling sounds from his basket as Melanie tickled him under the chin and arms and generally made a nuisance of herself. Eleanor's

Building BARNABY's BEDROOM

headache had grown worse too, and she'd come downstairs to find out what all that infernal banging was about. When she saw what her husband had done to the living-room ceiling, she stared at him, speechless, for a moment, wondering whether everyone in the house had gone quite mad.

"What on earth . . . ?" she asked, struggling for words, but Alistair simply smiled at her and brought the basket into the center of the living room, where he unclipped the rucksack cords to allow Barnaby to float upward once again. This time, however, he didn't bang his head against the ceiling and he didn't say "Ow." Instead, he had a much softer landing and seemed perfectly content to be left up there, playing with his fingers and examining his toes.

"It works," said Alistair in delight, turning to his wife, expecting her to be pleased by what he had done, but Eleanor, a perfectly normal woman, was aghast.

"It looks ridiculous," she cried.

"But it won't be for long," said Alistair. "Just until he settles down, that's all."

"But what if he never settles down? We can't leave him up there forever."

"Trust me, he'll get tired of all this floating business in due course," insisted Alistair, trying to be optimistic, despite the fact that he felt anything but. “Just wait, you’ll see. But until then we can’t have him bumping his head every time he gets away from us. He’ll damage his brain.”

Eleanor said nothing, just looked miserable. She lay down on the sofa and stared up at her son, stranded eleven feet above her, and wondered what she had ever done to deserve such a terrible misfortune. She was a perfectly normal woman, after all. She wasn’t the type to have a floating baby.

In the meantime, Alistair and Henry went about their business, installing the second mattress in the kitchen, directly over the place where Barnaby’s basket would be kept, and the third in his and Eleanor’s bedroom, for when he was asleep in his cot beside them at night.

“All done,” said Alistair, coming downstairs and finding Eleanor still lying on the sofa while Melanie sat on the floor next to her, reading *Heidi* for the seventeenth time. “Where’s Barnaby?”

Melanie pointed her index finger upward but uttered not a word; her eyes were pinned to the page. Peter the Goatherd was speaking and she wanted to hear his every syllable. That boy had wisdom beyond his years.

“Oh yes,” said Alistair, frowning, wondering what he should do next. “Do you think it’s all right to leave him up there for the rest of the day?”

Melanie continued to read until she reached

the end of a long paragraph, and then picked up her bookmark. She placed it carefully between pages 104 and 105 and set the novel on the cushion beside Eleanor before looking directly at her father. "You're asking me whether she should leave Barnaby on the ceiling of our living room for the rest of the day," she said coolly.

"Yes, that's right," said Alistair, unable to look his daughter in the eye.

"Barnaby," she repeated, "who is only a few days old. You want to know whether I think it's all right to just leave him stranded up there."

There was a long pause.

"I don't care for your tone," said Alistair eventually, his voice quiet and filled with shame.

"The answer to your question is no. No, I don't think it's all right to leave him up there like that."

"Well, then," said Alistair, reaching for a chair in order to retrieve the boy. "Perhaps you could have just said so."

At that moment the doorbell rang. It was Mr. Cody from next door looking for the keys to his van and, having received no immediate answer, marching in to retrieve them without so much as a by-your-leave. Alistair put Barnaby back in his basket but forgot to tie the straps, and in a moment the boy was on the ceiling once again, resting comfortably against the mattress.

Mr. Cody, who had lived a long time, fought in

two world wars, shaken the hand of Roald Dahl, and seen many unusual things across seven decades, some of which he had understood and some of which he hadn't, looked up and cocked his head to one side. He stroked his chin with one hand and ran his tongue slowly across his lips, first the upper lip, then the lower. Finally, shaking his head, he turned to Eleanor.

"That's not normal, that," he said, at which point Eleanor burst into tears and fled upstairs to throw herself on her bed, determined not to open her eyes lest she see the awful monstrosity of the third mattress pinned above her.

Chapter 3

Barnaby the Kite

When four years passed and nothing had changed, Barnaby's family had to accept that this wasn't a phase after all; it was just the way their son had been born. Alistair and Eleanor took him to a local doctor, who examined him thoroughly and suggested that they give him a couple of pills and call again in the morning, but this did nothing to improve matters. They took him to see an out-of-town specialist, who placed him on a course of antibiotics, but still he continued to float, although he became completely immune to a bad flu that was raging through Kirribilli that week. Finally, they drove him into the center of Sydney for an appointment with a famous consultant, who simply shook his head and said that the boy would grow out of it in time.

"Boys usually grow out of everything in the end," he said, smiling as he passed across a rather large invoice for the rather short time he'd spent examining Barnaby. "Their trousers. Their good behavior. Their willingness to respect parental authority. You simply have to be patient, that's all."

None of which helped Alistair or Eleanor in the least and, in fact, only served to frustrate them even more.

Now Barnaby slept in the lower bunk in Henry's room, where a couple of blankets had been stitched to the underside of his brother's bed to prevent him from hitting his head against the springs.

"It's nice to be able to see our ceiling again, isn't it?" said Alistair when the mattress in their bedroom was finally taken down. Eleanor nodded but said nothing. "It needs a fresh coat of paint, though," he added, filling the space left by her silence. "There's a great yellow square where the mattress used to be. You can make out the flower design."

There were a whole set of difficult circumstances associated with Barnaby's use of the bathroom, but perhaps it would be indelicate to go into them here. Suffice it to say that taking a shower was very difficult, a bath was out of the question, and using the toilet presented such a set of challenges that even a skilled contortionist would have found himself not quite up to the task.

In the evenings, when they would occasionally light up the barbecue for their evening meal, the family would sit around the garden table, Alistair,

Eleanor, Henry, and Melanie taking the four seats under the large sunshade while Barnaby hovered beneath its pointed peak, prevented from drifting off into the atmosphere by the strong green canvas that held him in place. He was banned from putting tomato ketchup on his hot dogs or burgers, as it had a terrible habit of falling down on one or all of their heads.

"But I like tomato ketchup," Barnaby would complain, thinking this was most unfair. He could, of course, say more than "Ow" by now.

"And I prefer not to have to shampoo my hair every day," replied his father.

At such times, Captain W. E. Johns would sit on the ground staring up at the boy, awaiting instructions; the dog had decided that this floating child was his sole master and would take direction from no other.

But the days were often rather boring. Eleanor had given up work shortly after Melanie's birth, so she and Barnaby were left alone together for great stretches of time with only Captain W. E. Johns to act as a buffer between them. They almost never left the house during daylight hours, as Eleanor did not want to be seen in public with her son in case people pointed and stared. Alistair too refused to take Barnaby with him when he strolled across to Kirribilli market on a Saturday morning, browsing through the stalls for a bargain, as he knew that he would inevitably become the exact type of person he had always despised: somebody different.

Because of this, Barnaby grew into an unusually pale child, as he almost never saw direct sunlight. For a time, Eleanor would tie him to the washing line on the back lawn and let him hover in the fresh air for a couple of hours. When there was a breeze, he might even rotate for an afternoon, ensuring an even tan. Eventually, however, she was forced to put a stop to this, as there were several extravagant bird feeders placed in different areas of the garden, and a four-year-old boy tied by his ankles to a washing line and waving his arms around in the air like a lunatic made him seem more like a scarecrow than anything else and the birds stopped coming.

"He's as white as a ghost," said Alistair, looking up at his son one evening as they were eating dinner.

"Almost as white as our ceilings used to be," remarked Eleanor. "Before they had mattresses nailed to them."

"It can't be good for him, though, can it?"

"We've discussed this, Alistair," said Eleanor with a sigh, resting her fork on the side of her plate. "If we take him outside, what will the neighbors think? They might even suspect that we all float behind closed doors."

"Oh, really, Eleanor," said Alistair, laughing at

the idea. "I've never floated in my life, you know that. I keep my feet firmly on the ground."

"And there are the other children to think of," she added. "What if the boys in Henry's class, for example, hear about Barnaby and think that Henry floats too? They might stop being friends with him."

"I'm sure they wouldn't. It's not a *choice* that Barnaby's made, after all. It's just the way he was born."

"Tell that to Henry when he's being beaten up in the schoolyard."

"I don't think that would—"

"Children can be very cruel," she continued, ignoring her husband's interruption. "And, anyway, it's easier to keep him under control here in the house. Think what might happen if we took him outside. He could simply float away and we'd never see him again."

As she said this, she was bringing a forkful of lasagna to her mouth, but it hovered in midair before reaching her lips; for a moment she realized how much easier life would be if this was to happen. Alistair glanced at her, and something passed between them—the germ of a terrible idea that remained unspoken. For now.

"Anyway, if you're so concerned, you could always take him out when you come home from work," she said a moment later.

"Out of the question," replied Alistair instantly, shaking his head as if the very idea needed to be rattled out of his brain and his ears before it did any damage. "I will not, repeat *not,* make myself a figure of ridicule among our neighbors."

"Well, then, don't expect *me* to."

"Perhaps we could hire someone?" suggested Alistair. "Like a professional dog walker."

"But then we would have to explain his condition to a stranger. And before you know it, the gossips would be out in force."

"True. But what about school?"

"What *about* school?" asked Eleanor, frowning. "What do you mean? He doesn't go to school."

"Not yet he doesn't, no. But soon he will. He's supposed to start in a few months' time. If he goes in as white as that, everyone will think there's something wrong with him."

"There *is* something wrong with him, Alistair."

"I mean, they'll think he has a skin disease and no one will want to sit next to him. And before you know it, the school authorities will drag us all in to meet the nurse, and who knows what trouble that will cause. They might put it in the newsletter, and then everyone will know that I have fathered a floating boy. No, I'm sorry, Eleanor, but I'm putting my foot down."

"You're doing *what*?" asked Eleanor incredulously.

"I'm putting my foot down," he repeated in a more forceful voice. "I am head of this household, and I have decided that we'll have to risk all the ugly stares and cruel gossip. The boy must be brought out into direct sunlight. You can get the ball rolling tomorrow morning when you take Captain W. E. Johns for his walk."

The dog's tail wagged at this most wonderful of words—a single syllable that offered unparalleled delights—and Eleanor, too exhausted to offer any more resistance, reluctantly agreed. And so, the following morning—a bright, sunny day, perfect for putting a little color into a pale boy's cheeks—she clapped her hands to summon Captain W. E. Johns, clipping his lead onto his collar before ascending a kitchen chair to take Barnaby down off the ceiling.

"We're going for a walk," she told him in a matter-of-fact voice.

"Around the house?"

"No, outside."

"Outside?" asked Barnaby, who hadn't for a moment believed that his mother would do what his father had insisted on the night before.

"That's right. But before we go—well, I'm sorry about this but there's something I've got to do."

And with that she retrieved Captain W. E. Johns's spare collar, which had an expandable neck, and the second lead, which they kept in the kitchen drawer, and a few minutes later all three were on their way.

They made an extraordinary sight as they set off from their home in Kirribilli, making their way along the street that led toward the governor-general's house at the southernmost point of the peninsula: a middle-aged woman walking along with her head bowed low in shame, a dog of indeterminate breed and parentage trotting a few feet ahead of her as she held his lead in her left hand, while a four-year-old boy, white as a ghost, hovered above them both, suspended in the air by the lead she held in her right.

Barnaby Brocket had become a kite.

They made their way north toward St. Aloysius' College, where Henry was coming to the end of year five, but once the bell rang and the children could be heard running down the stairs inside, Eleanor turned and walked quickly toward the Jeffrey Street Wharf, where she liked to stand and look across the water at the sails of the Opera House, the sweep of the skyscrapers, and the hotels dotted between them. The Harbour Bridge stood proudly to her right, linking the shores of North Sydney to The Rocks beyond, and she turned to it, staring up toward the flags floating in the breeze, before breathing in deeply and feeling, for a moment at least, at peace.

"Morning, Eleanor!" called Mr. Chappaqua, a

going for a walk

former Olympic twenty-kilometer racewalker—Montreal, nineteen seventy-six; fourth place—who passed her at this time every day from the direction of Beulah Street, where he always began his morning constitutional, elbows tucked into his body as he waddled along like a duck in a baseball cap. "Good morning, Captain W. E. Johns!"

And then, looking up, he noticed Barnaby floating above her, and his cheerful expression immediately changed. Mr. Chappaqua was Sydney-born and -bred. He took great pride in the city, its people, and its fine traditions. He'd even stood for a parliament seat a few years before—fourth place once again—and remained a regular letter writer to the *Sydney Morning Herald*, where he complained about anything that wasn't in keeping with his standards, which were exceptionally high.

"Your boy is floating, Mrs. Brocket," he said, appalled, unable to bear the familiarity of her first name now. "He's *floating*!"

"Is he?" asked Eleanor, looking up as if this was a tremendous surprise to her.

"You know he is. You have him on a leash! Is this where we're headed now, Mrs. Brocket? Are these the depths to which Sydney, the most magnificent city in the world, has sunk?"

Eleanor opened her mouth to defend herself but could find no words to explain her son's behavior, and Mr. Chappaqua, dismayed, simply growled like a roused wolf and marched straight home to Mrs. Chappaqua, who suggested that where there was one, there would surely be more, and before long Sydney would be overrun by the nasty creatures.

And although Eleanor felt humiliated by this encounter, Barnaby was too enraptured by the wonderful new sights that were on display before him to care. He looked down at Captain W. E. Johns, who, sensing his master's excitement, wagged his tail in delight. He squinted in the bright morning as the sun reflected off the water, inspiring rainbows of color to spring from the waves. Watching one of the ferries making its way from Circular Quay round the curve toward Neutral Bay, Barnaby wished that he could be on board, that he could see what existed even farther away in those places he had never been allowed to visit.

"I knew this was a bad idea," said Eleanor furiously, turning round and heading back in the direction from which they had come. "We'll be the talk of the neighborhood now. The sooner I get you back indoors, Barnaby, the better."

But as they made their way along the street toward home, they were met by another neighbor, or rather a pair of neighbors, named Joe and Alice Moffat, who were something big in computers (or so Eleanor had heard). They were chatting away quite happily as they walked along, hand in hand, but when they saw Eleanor, Barnaby, and Captain W. E.

Johns coming their way, they immediately stopped and stared, their mouths falling open in surprise.

"I have to get a picture of this," said Joe Moffat, pulling a smartphone from his pocket and aiming it at Barnaby. He was a dirty young man who always had a messy sort of half beard on his face and wore nothing but T-shirts, shorts, and thongs on his feet despite the fact that he was rumored to be worth in the region of a billion Australian dollars. "Hey, Mrs. Brocket! Stand still, will you? I'm trying to get a picture of your boy."

"I will not stand still, you degenerate animal," snapped Eleanor, rushing past him and almost knocking his wife over as she did so, moving at such a speed that Barnaby felt a great breeze in his face—a breeze so strong that his hair blew backward and provided a sort of windbreaker for the three of them, serving only to slow them down, which was an irony of sorts. "And please stop staring at me—it's extremely rude."

"Just one picture, please," said Joe, running after her. "Everyone will want to see this."

I wouldn't like to tell you what Eleanor said then, but it wasn't nice, and she sprinted all the way home, delighting Captain W. E. Johns, who loved a decent run, but leaving poor Barnaby shivering with the cold. Safely back indoors, she unclipped the lead from the dog's collar, and he immediately ran out into the back garden on private business. Then she unclipped the other lead from around Barnaby's neck and let him float back up toward his David Jones Bellissimo plush medium mattress.

"This is unacceptable behavior," she shouted up at him, wagging her finger and feeling such resentment now toward the little boy that the bad ideas were returning to her mind. "I won't have it, Barnaby Brocket, do you hear me? I am your mother and I insist that you stop floating this instant. Come down here!"

"But I can't," said Barnaby in a sad voice.

"Come down here!" she shouted, her face growing red with fury now.

"I don't know how to," said Barnaby. "It's just who I am."

"Then I'm sorry," said Eleanor, shaking her head and lowering her voice at last. "But I have to say that I don't like who you are very much."

And with that she went into the kitchen, closed the door behind her, and didn't speak to anyone again for the rest of the afternoon.

Chapter 4

The Best Day of Barnaby's Life So Far

"St. Aloysius' is the obvious choice," said Eleanor, the evening she and Alistair were deciding what to do about Barnaby's education. "It's only down the road, after all."

"I'm not sending him there," said Alistair. "Most of our neighbors send their sons to that school. Everyone in Kirribilli will be talking about us. And what if it gets back to Bother & Blastit? People might look at me funnily."

"Well, where do you suggest, then?" asked Eleanor.

"What's the name of that school on Lavender Bay? It's a little farther away but—"

"Absolutely not!" said Eleanor, looking at her husband as if he had no more sense than a rabbit. "Jane Macquarie-Hamid across the street sends her little Duncan there. What would she say?"

"Well, I don't know what other choices we have," replied Alistair with a sigh. "We could always keep him at home, I suppose. Does he really need an education, after all?"

"Oh, of course he does," said Eleanor, scrolling through a list of Sydney schools on the Internet until she found one that satisfied her needs. "We can't add ignorance and stupidity to his other failings. Now look, here we are," she added triumphantly, spinning the laptop round to show her husband. "The Graveling Academy for Unwanted Children."

"It's almost as if it was built with Barnaby in mind," said Alistair, examining the school's website, which made a great deal of the fact that it had been set up by a former governor of Dillwynia Women's Correctional Centre to educate those children who, for one reason or another, had been rejected by the regular school system.

"Shall I make an appointment?"

"It couldn't do any harm to visit. Anyway, it looks rather nice, doesn't it?" he added, clicking through the photos on the computer screen. "All that barbed wire on top of the walls is probably there as part of a project to teach the children about prisoner-of-war camps."

"And the look of the building itself," said Eleanor. "It's like one of those workhouses out of *Oliver Twist*. The children must love it!"

"They certainly must," agreed Alistair, and so, three days later, they found themselves sitting in front of Harriet Hooperman-Hall, the school principal.

"It's not that he's not an intelligent little boy," said Alistair.

"He's actually very bright," said Eleanor. "He reads the most extraordinary books. He prefers authors who are dead," she added, laughing a little, as if she had never heard of such an extraordinary thing.

"And he's never been in any trouble," said Alistair. "But we do feel that Barnaby would benefit from some—how shall I put this?—special attention."

Mrs. Hooperman-Hall smiled and stroked her whiskers; she looked a little like a female goat, although her two front teeth resembled those of a dromedary. Before speaking, she ran her tongue along the thick, gloopy layer of dark red lipstick that stuck to the edges of her mouth like mortar to a brick, and snaked it in and out in a rather disgusting fashion.

"Alistair and Eleanor," she said. "Or may I call you Mr. and Mrs. Brocket? We at the Graveling Academy have long suffered from a misunderstanding that our students are more difficult than those in other schools. Yes, it's true that some of our pupils have been in and out of young offenders' institutions since before they could walk. And, yes, it's an unfortunate fact that we have security cameras in every classroom and metal detectors over every door. And, no, we don't go in for any of that modern mumbo-jumbo that requires all our teachers to be 'board-certified,' whatever that means. I've never actually understood that term, have you?"

"Well, I think it means—"

"But despite all these things, we pride ourselves on the fact that we open our doors at eight o'clock every morning and padlock them shut again every afternoon at three. And while nothing of very much use happens in the eight hours in between—"

"I think that's seven hours, actually," said Alistair, who had always been good with numbers.

"While nothing of very much use happens in the eight hours in between," insisted Mrs. Hooperman-Hall, "we do at least keep the children out of your way—which, let's face it, is what you're looking for. We embrace difference here," she added in a magnanimous tone. "So your little Barnaby floats. What matter? We have a child of six who hops like a kangaroo. Another who held up a liquor store in an armed robbery and refuses to say where she stashed the loot. A third who speaks French fluently. But do we hold any of these things against them? No, we do not."

Which was good enough for Alistair and Eleanor, and shortly after this, they left the school, trying not to notice how the wallpaper was peeling off the walls, the carpets were covered in cigarette burns, and the overflowing wastepaper baskets next to them were quite clearly a fire hazard.

Having had little contact with other children during his short life—except for Henry and Melanie, of course—Barnaby was understandably nervous during his first week at the Graveling Academy for Unwanted Children. Fortunately for him, however, he was placed next to another new boy, Liam McGonagall, whose great-great-great-grandfather had been one of the first convicts to be shipped to Australia from Britain during the 1800s, having already been exported from Ireland for taking a pee on a statue of King George IV. Like Barnaby, Liam found the idea of spending the day with a classroom full of children he'd never met before intimidating; he too had failed to make friends, having been born with an unfortunate medical abnormality: his arms came to an end at the wrists and he had two neat sets of steel hooks where his hands should have been. These terrified most of the other children in the class but didn't bother Barnaby in the slightest. In fact, he would have made a point of shaking Liam's right hook on the first morning they met and every morning afterward, only this was impossible, for Mrs. Hooperman-Hall always collected him at the front door and brought him directly to his seat,

meeting Liam

tying him to his chair with a strong rope and a series of complicated knots.

"Was it an accident?" he asked Liam when they became friendly enough to ask personal questions, which was only a few hours later. "The loss of your hands, I mean."

"No, I was born like this," said Liam. "It was just one of those things. Some people have no brain, like Denis Lickton over there." He nodded toward a taller-than-average boy who was engaged in a conversation with his shoes. "Some have no sense of style," he continued, glancing at a nervous-looking chap, George Raftery, who wore a Robin Hood–type hat on his head. "But me, I have no hands. I tried false ones for a while but I couldn't get used to them. The hooks work better. I can do anything with my hooks. Except pick my nose."

"They're very shiny," said Barnaby, admiring the way they sparkled.

"That's because I polish them every morning before leaving the house," said Liam, pleased that Barnaby had noticed. "I like to look good. Anyway, I've never known anything different, so they don't bother me at all. Except I can't play basketball, and I bet I'd be good at it."

"I'd be brilliant at it," said Barnaby. "All I'd have to do with the ball is float up and drop it in the basket. I'd score every time."

"Have you always floated?"

"Since the day I was born."

"Well, good on you!" said Liam McGonagall, and that was all it took to become friends. Simple, really.

As the weeks passed, the daily routine remained the same. Barnaby arrived at the Graveling Academy just before the starting pistol was sounded and was immediately tied into his chair and left there for the rest of the day, while he did his best not to get too upset when the other boys picked on him, all the time forging a happy friendship with Liam McGonagall.

"Do you like it at your new school?" Alistair asked him one evening over dinner, looking up at his son as they finished off a rhubarb flan that Eleanor had been working on all afternoon and was almost, but not quite, palatable.

"No, it's horrible," said Barnaby. "The place smells like rotten fruit, the other children are mean to me, and we're never taught anything real. Today we spent an hour studying the kings and queens of New Zealand, learned how to plant potato trees, and were told that the capital city of Italy is Jupiter."

"It's Barcelona, isn't it?" asked Alistair, who might have been very good with numbers but had a bit of a blind spot when it came to geography. (He'd never left Australia, of course, believing that normal people shouldn't want to see the world. In fact, he'd never even left the state of New South Wales. For that matter, he'd never even left Sydney.)

"Mrs. Hooperman-Hall then said that she wanted to start a book club and asked if we had any suggestions for what we might read. I said *The Man in the Iron Mask,* and she told me that, no, books like that were far too complicated for her and she wouldn't be able to sleep if her head was full of conspiracy theories. So then I suggested *Bobby Brewster Bus Conductor,* and she said she really only wanted to read books about vampires because they were all so stimulating and original."

"What does *stimulating* mean?" asked Melanie, looking up. Henry snorted into his flan and Captain W. E. Johns allowed his ears to fall over his face.

"Melanie!" snapped Eleanor, appalled. "Do not use that word. I will not have anybody being stimulated in this house, do you hear me? It's not normal."

"I've never been stimulated in my life," added Alistair. "And I'm in my forties."

"I hate that school," muttered Barnaby. "There's only one boy there who I get along with. He has a set of hooks where his hands should be."

"Excellent," remarked Henry.

"It's not excellent," insisted Eleanor, shaking her head as if she expected nothing less from a school that would accept her son as a student. "It's abnormal, that's what it is. But still, I'm glad you're happy there."

"But I'm not happy there," said Barnaby. "I just told you that."

"That's nice, dear."

But, as things turned out, his career at the Graveling Academy would come to an abrupt end anyway. The following Wednesday afternoon the rotten smell, the greasy ceilings, the overflowing wastepaper baskets, the cigarette burns, Mrs. Hooperman-Hall's lipstick, and the peeling wallpaper all combined to start a spontaneous flame in the corner of the long corridor that separated the newest students, still on probation, from the lifers. The fire trickled along the ancient carpets, giving birth to a number of smaller flames as it licked its way under each door, and once inside Barnaby's classroom, it quickly climbed the walls, finding fuel to help it grow bigger and stronger at every turn. Within a few minutes, Mrs. Hooperman-Hall and the children were screaming and pulling the ancient steel bars off the windows, jumping out onto the roof, and shinnying down the drainpipe to safety.

Barnaby was still tied to his chair, however. No one had even thought of saving him.

"Help!" he cried, pulling at his cords, but the more he did so, the tighter they became. "Help me, someone!"

A BAD Day
at SCHOOL

The flames were growing larger now, and one entire wall of the classroom was eaten up by fire. Barnaby started to cough, feeling the smoke getting caught up in his throat and choking him as his eyes began to stream with tears.

"Help!" he cried again, his voice barely audible now. He realized that this might be the last word he ever spoke, that he would die here in the fire and never see Alistair, Eleanor, Henry, Melanie, or Captain W. E. Johns again. He gave one more mighty pull on the ropes around his wrists and ankles, but nothing he did could make them loosen. Looking down, he realized that it would be impossible to set himself free and that he would have to face up to the next horrible few minutes with as much bravery as he could muster. Even if someone came back for him now, the knots had been pulled too tight for any human hands to unpick them.

Which is why it was very lucky that the only person who came to help Barnaby didn't have human hands at all: he had a rather fine set of hooks instead.

"Sit still, Barnaby," cried Liam McGonagall, coughing too and trying to keep his eyes focused on the ropes as he used the tips in a pincer movement to undo the knots. "Stop pulling at them—you're making it even harder for me."

Barnaby did as he was told and soon began to

feel a definite looseness round his left ankle; in a moment he was able to pull his leg free. Then another at his right. Then his left arm, followed quickly by his right. Liam had done it—he had untied the knots.

"Oh no you don't," he said, locking his hooks around Barnaby's ankles as his friend started to float up toward the ceiling, which was a flaming orange sea of fire by now. "Jump on my back, Barnaby, and hold on tight."

Barnaby did as he was told, and the two boys made their way toward the window, jumped out, and slid down the drainpipe, landing on the ground with an almighty bump that knocked them off their feet. Barnaby came very close to floating away again, only Liam was too quick for him and made sure to keep a tight hold.

"There she goes," said Barnaby, looking up at the ancient building as it gave in to the flames and collapsed in upon itself.

"They'll never be able to reopen it now," said Liam.

The two boys looked at each other and broke into wide smiles. It was probably the best day of Barnaby Brocket's life so far.

Chapter 5

The Magician on the Bridge

Two weeks later, Barnaby was tied to the living-room sofa reading Robert Louis Stevenson's *Kidnapped* when Eleanor walked in, dragging behind her a heavy parcel with a tag attached that read: *For Barnaby, from Eleanor Brocket (Mrs.).*

"For me?" he asked, looking up at his mother in surprise.

"Yes, it's a special present," she told him. "You'll like it, I promise."

Barnaby pulled the wrapping paper off to discover a brand-new rucksack inside. It was a little too large for his small body and had a pair of strong shoulder straps dangling from the side.

"It's for school," said Eleanor, who had given up trying to find a school that none of her friends might have heard of and had settled, reluctantly, for a local primary.

"But I already have a bag," he said.

"Yes, but that's to keep all your schoolbooks in.

This one, this new one . . . ," explained Eleanor. "Well, just put it on your back and you'll see what it's for."

Barnaby reached down to pick it up and, to his great surprise, found that it was almost impossible to lift. "It's so heavy," he said. "It feels like it's full of rocks."

"Don't worry about that," said Eleanor as Captain W. E. Johns drifted into the living room to check on his master. "Just put it on, all right? I want to see whether it works or not."

Barnaby struggled to lift the bag off the ground, but eventually he managed to get his left shoulder into one of the straps. He almost fell over when he did so, but somehow he managed to get his right arm in too, and then everything balanced out. His feet hovered off the ground for a few seconds and he started to float, but after a moment the weight of the bag was too much for him and he came back down to the floor, his shoes landing on the carpet with a satisfying thump.

Captain W. E. Johns, dissatisfied, barked.

"It works!" cried Eleanor, clapping her hands together in delight. "I got some sandbags from the council after I told them that I was worried about flooding. I put two inside to balance out your weight. It's perfect, isn't it?"

"But I won't be able to walk with this on my back," protested Barnaby. "It hurts too much."

"Oh, don't be such a baby."

Barnaby, anxious to please, did as he was told, but it wasn't easy. During the first week his shoulders turned black-and-blue from the weight that he was being forced to carry, but in time they grew stronger and he didn't notice it quite so much. As every month passed and he grew a little more, Eleanor put extra sand in the bag and the whole painful process began all over again. The curious thing, however, was that whenever he was forced to stay on the ground, his ears hurt a little.

In the classroom, Barnaby's ankles were secured to his chair by a pair of handcuffs and he was able to keep his hands and body free in case an important visitor, like the prime minister or one of the Minogue sisters, happened to stop by on an official visit; the school, like Alistair and Eleanor, was not keen on anyone who stood out from the crowd.

The only thing that made Barnaby sad was that his friend, Liam McGonagall, had not been sent to the same school. His family had moved to India, where his father had been offered a job designing computer accessories, and they fell out of touch, as sometimes even the closest of friends do.

A year passed, and then another, and then two more, and Barnaby turned eight. He still slept in the lower bunk in Henry's room and had been given the top shelf of the bookcase in order to store his growing library. It made a lot of sense, as he could float around the ceilings as much as he liked, reorganizing the volumes, moving all his *Three Musketeers* books into one place and keeping his treasured orphan collection—*Oliver Twist, The Cider House Rules, Jane Eyre*—close at hand.

Barnaby Brocket felt a special affinity with orphans.

And then, one fine February morning, his teacher, Mr. Pelford, announced to the students that they were leaving the school grounds on a special excursion.

"What's the most famous attraction in Sydney?" he asked, looking around the room for the sea of hands that never appeared. "Katherine Flowers?"

"The Westfield mall?" she said, shrugging her shoulders.

"Don't be ridiculous," snapped Mr. Pelford. "Stupid girl. Marcus Foot, the most famous attraction in Sydney, please?"

"The Opera House," replied the boy, who had seen a play there once and had dreamed ever since of playing a great Shakespearean hero on the Opera House stage. Preferably someone who wore tights and carried a sword. Marcus Foot, an unusual boy in many respects, thought there could be nothing better in life than prancing about in a pair of tights while brandishing a sword.

"Yes, but that's not the one I'm thinking of," said Mr. Pelford. "Come on, someone else, please. Someone with a brain in their head."

"The Great Wall of China," offered Richard L'Estrange.

"The Niagara Falls," said Emily Piper.

"Big Ben," shouted the Mickleson twins, Amy and Aimee.

"For heaven's sake, children," said the teacher, throwing his hands in the air. "It's the Harbour Bridge, of course. An extraordinary feat of engineering, at the top of which, I might add, one Geena Llewellyn agreed to become the second Mrs. David Pelford on a rainy July afternoon some seven years ago."

The children looked a little skeptical that Mr. Pelford could possibly have persuaded one person to marry him, let alone two.

"And as a special treat," he continued, "I've arranged for us all to climb the bridge this afternoon, like the tourists do. Yes, even you, Stephen Hebden. I don't want to hear a word about your chronic vertigo."

Happy to do something different, the children made their way outside to the waiting bus, and on the short journey that followed, Barnaby looked down from the ceiling as the other children read comics, examined the contents of their handkerchiefs, or listened to their iPods, and wished that he could take the empty seat among them that was rightfully his.

When they reached the bridge, they were met by a young student named Darren—"Call me Daz"—who had messy blond hair, a sunburned face, and the whitest teeth Barnaby had ever seen on a human being.

"Good morning, bridge climbers!" he shouted, looking as if he had never been quite as happy as he was at that very moment. "Is everyone ready to see Sydney from above?"

There were a few grunts from the children, which Daz seemed to take as assent, because he clapped his hands together and roared, "Well, all right, then!" in a hysterical tone. In fact, some of Barnaby's classmates were starting to grow very enthusiastic now as the great expanse of the bridge appeared before them. Most of them had driven back and forth across it in their parents' cars hundreds of times, but they had never really looked at it before. And for some, for those observant few, it was a thing of beauty.

"Of course we can't climb in our civvies," said Daz, leading them into a special chamber where a row of gray-and-blue jumpsuits were laid out for them, along with caps, fleeces, rain jackets, special climbing shoes, and a bundle of curious-looking cables. "We've got to look the part."

They got dressed, each one enjoying the feeling

of being bundled up in such fantastic new gear, and the girls gathered their hair up in specially provided scrunchies, so it wouldn't blow in their faces. "It can get pretty windy up there," said Daz, laughing happily, as if the prospect of being blown over the side into the harbor waters was a terrific joke. "And we don't want anyone falling in, do we? Never again, that's my motto! Now, anyone been drinking?"

The children looked at each other in confusion, and Marcus Foot raised his hand tentatively. "I had a black-currant cordial in the bus," he said nervously. "But I've already been to the bathroom, if that's what you're worried about."

"I've been four times," said Stephen Hebden, who was looking for any excuse to avoid the climb.

"Not soft drinks," said Daz, laughing. "Grog! We can't have anyone climbing the bridge if they've been on the sauce. I need everyone to take a Breathalyzer test."

"For heaven's sake," said Mr. Pelford, momentarily worried that he himself might not pass it. "They're only eight years old."

"Regulations, mate," said Daz, getting each child to blow into a tube and examining the reading. "More than my job's worth to let anyone go up without blowing in here first."

Ten minutes later, when all had proved sober, a collection of cords and wires were attached to their suits in complicated ways and they were led out to the iron steps. The moment he got outside, Barnaby started to float upward, only slightly held down by the weight of the suit and the equipment he was carrying, but Daz was too quick for him, grabbing him by the ankle and pulling him back to the ground.

"Where do you think you're going, mate?" he asked, staring at the boy in surprise.

"It's not my fault," explained Barnaby. "I float."

"Well, that's crackin'!" roared Daz, who was one of those rare people who embraced difference rather than feared it. He held on to Barnaby as he arranged all the children in single file, then locked the harnesses of their suits to the pole that ran along the inside of the bridge itself.

"You know, we're not supposed to take kids as young as you climbing," Daz told them when they were just about to start. "But today is a very special day."

"Why's that?" asked George Jones, a boy who was known for his flatulence—a reputation that, a moment later, he justified.

"It just is, mate," said Daz, winking at him. "Think of me as the magician on the bridge. All will be revealed in time."

They began to ascend and, connected to the bridge, Barnaby found himself able to walk without anyone holding him down.

"You're just like the rest of us now," said Philip Wensleydale, grinning at him.

"Yes," replied Barnaby, frowning so much that a little vertical crease appeared in the gap between his eyebrows. "Yes, I suppose I am."

Only, to his great surprise, Barnaby didn't enjoy feeling like the rest of them. It was as if he was pretending to be someone he wasn't.

They made their way up, and one girl, Jeannie Jenkins, tried to start a sing-along with a rousing rendition of "Advance Australia Fair," but no one joined in and she gave up after the first verse. Donald Sutcliffe and his mortal enemy James Caruthers, stuck one in front of the other, began a conversation about their dogs, both of whom were Cavalier King Charles spaniels; they quickly forgot all the terrible things they had done to each other over the years and forged a new friendship. Katie Lynch, a studious girl, recited poetry in her head. Cornelius Hastings, known to everyone as "Corny," looked over the side and pointed at every building he saw, gasping in astonishment and saying "I should have brought my camera" over and over, until Lisa Farragher, directly behind him, threatened him with violence. Dylan Cotter counted the steps. Jean Kavanagh played with her hair. Anne Griffin wondered whether the man who lived next door to her might have murdered his recently deceased wife and decided that when she returned to ground level, she would begin an investigation.

In short, everyone kept busy as they made their way up the side of the Harbour Bridge.

After about an hour, they reached the top and turned round to look down at the city spread out before them. It was an extraordinary sight. In the distance, a hot-air balloon was coming in to land on one of the green areas beyond the city, and Barnaby could just make out two figures inside the basket, jumping up and down in delight. Beneath them, the lanes of traffic were whizzing across from one side of Sydney to the other, the noise of the engines drowning out the sound of Stephen Hebden's screams and George Jones's farting. To their right, they could see almost as far as Cockatoo Island, and when Barnaby turned to his left, he was looking down on the white tiles of the Opera House and the ferries shuttling the Sydneysiders from Circular Quay to the bays and coves beyond.

Standing there, it was easy to see why Sydney really was the most magnificent city in the world, and Barnaby knew that only a fool would choose to live anywhere else.

"Right, down we go," announced Daz after they'd taken some photographs, and the entire group turned to begin their descent.

Halfway down, Barnaby noticed that a great crowd had gathered at the bridge's entrance platform;

when they got closer, he could make out a group of news vans with satellite dishes on top parked outside on the street and a crowd of photographers taking pictures from the terrace of the Harbour View Hotel.

"What's going on?" asked Lucy Honeyfield.

"I told you it was a special day," said Daz, smiling but refusing to give any more details. When they reached the base, a line of people were gathered on either side to welcome them, standing in two rows like ball boys in the guard of honor at the Rod Laver Arena.

"Nine million nine hundred and ninety-nine thousand nine hundred and ninety-seven," they called out in one voice—which wasn't easy—as Dennis Peel walked between them and unhooked himself from the bridge.

"Nine million nine hundred and ninety-nine thousand nine hundred and ninety-eight," they cried when Emily Piper followed him.

"Nine million nine hundred and ninety-nine thousand nine hundred and ninety-nine," they shouted, their voices rising now in excitement as Jeannie Jenkins stepped off.

And then—

"TEN MILLION!" they roared as Barnaby Brocket placed his foot on the bottom step, and a sudden flurry of cameramen and photographers jostled with reporters for the best position.

9,999,994....

9,999,995...

9,999,996...

"What's your name, son?" asked a middle-aged man in a striped tweed suit, shoving a microphone under his mouth with a square attachment that read CHANNEL 9 NEWS.

"Barnaby Brocket," said Barnaby Brocket.

"And what does it feel like to be the ten millionth person to climb the Sydney Harbour Bridge?"

Barnaby looked around, a little dazzled by the attention, and Daz came over, unhooked his chain, and lifted him onto his shoulders before he could float away. He brought him inside to where a press conference was about to begin, and sat him on a chair next to an extremely elderly man who slapped his hand down on Barnaby's knee and held it there firmly as he scrunched up his face and peered at the boy.

"I'm the last one alive," he said.

"The last what alive?" asked Barnaby.

"I built the bridge," said the old man. "Not single-handed, of course, but as good as."

And with that, he released his hand and Barnaby floated upward and was left stranded on the ceiling. The room immediately became a lightning storm of flashbulbs and television cameras.

"Amazing!" cried the journalists.

"Extraordinary!"

"Horrible, utterly horrible!"

This last cry didn't come from anyone at the

press conference, but from Eleanor Brocket as she watched the news later that night.

"They think he's a freak. They think we're *all* freaks!" She turned to her husband in despair and looked out of the front window, where news vans had been gathered since the late afternoon. "He's making a mockery of our family. The whole thing is mortifying."

"You simply can't be trusted, can you?" snapped Alistair, wagging his finger up at his son, who was pressed against his David Jones Bellissimo plush medium mattress on the ceiling. "Look at all the unwelcome attention you've brought our way. How many times do we have to tell you?"

"But it wasn't my fault," protested Barnaby.

"Oh, it's always your fault," insisted Alistair. "I was at work—*at work,* Barnaby!—and your antics appeared on the television. Do you have any idea what that was like for me? Everyone looking in my direction? Whispering about me? Talking about me behind my back?"

"I'm sorry," said Barnaby, feeling tears beginning to form behind his eyes.

"What good is *sorry*?" said Alistair, turning away and sitting down, burying his face in his hands. "All I ever wanted was to live a normal life, with a normal family and normal children. And then you came along and ruined everything."

Eleanor looked at her husband and understood

his anger, for she felt it in equal measure. Staring up at her son, she breathed heavily through her nose like a dragon preparing to incinerate a group of untidy villagers and spoke with barely controlled rage.

"We will *not* put up with this a moment longer," she declared. "Eight years is eight years too many. We will not have a son who is different—do you understand me, Barnaby? Something has to be done. Either you become normal or . . . or . . ." She thought about it, wondering how she could finish this sentence. "Or we will put an end to your selfishness once and for all ourselves."

Chapter 6

The Terrible Thing That Happened at Mrs. Macquarie's Chair

It was almost a week before the journalists and news crews grew tired of sitting outside the Brocket house and went away to bother other people instead. Eleanor hadn't dared to venture outside during all that time but had brooded indoors instead, saying little, her resentment toward Barnaby growing all the time. Alistair had taken a few days off work, something he had never done before, as normal people, he announced, didn't call in sick; they worked five days a week, nine to five, and undertook a fair day's work for a fair day's pay. Finally, on a gloomy Thursday night, they sat in the kitchen together with the door closed. Henry and Melanie were sent to their rooms. Barnaby was left floating on the mattress in the living room. Even Captain W. E. Johns was exiled to the garden, despite the fact that he had conducted his private business earlier in a concealed area behind an apple tree and had nothing further to add.

Eleanor began the conversation, telling Alistair about an idea that had come to her recently. (Actually, it hadn't come to her recently at all; it had come to her in the back of the taxi cab eight years earlier when she was returning from the hospital, but she didn't want to admit that.)

Alistair thought that her idea had some merit but suggested a few changes of his own.

Eleanor agreed to these changes and added a few more, one of which they agreed to discard as being unnecessary and only there for comic effect.

Alistair threw in one final proposal, and Eleanor ran to the kitchen drawer to make sure that her sharpest pair of steel scissors could be found in the usual place.

"They're here," she said, holding them up and letting the light from the setting sun, which was coming through the window, gleam off the blades in a satisfactory manner.

And it was then that their terrible decision was reached.

"Are we sure about this?" asked Eleanor.

"I'm sure if you're sure," said Alistair.

"Yes," said Eleanor decisively. "I'm one hundred percent sure."

"There'll be no turning back, you understand that?"

"Alistair, he has no one to blame but himself. Did you put your parents through this nightmare? Did I?"

"Should we shake on it?" asked Alistair, extending his hand.

"I don't think so," replied Eleanor, unwilling to engage in such a common act. "We're not underworld criminals."

The following morning broke with a burst of sunshine and a group of six red-eyed common koels making temporary nests in the Brocket garden, much to the displeasure of Captain W. E. Johns, who guarded his patch with an authority not seen since the heyday of the Roman centurions. The family was gathered in the kitchen as usual, finishing breakfast, the children full of beans, the parents unusually subdued.

"Barnaby's not wearing his uniform," said Melanie, looking up at the ceiling. "Isn't he going back to school today?"

"Not today, dear, no," replied Eleanor.

"But all the reporters have left. His brain will grow soggy if he sits around the house much longer."

"We'll decide that, young lady," said Alistair. "Not you."

"And we have decided," said Eleanor, staring fiercely at her husband, wanting to be absolutely certain that there were no faint hearts this morning. "Haven't we?"

"Yes," replied Alistair. "I can confidently say that this is the best decision I've ever made in my life."

"That's a little over the top, don't you think?" asked Melanie, looking at her father in surprise. "All you're doing is keeping Barnaby off school for another day."

"Everyone in my class thinks Barnaby's brilliant," remarked Henry, reaching across for one more piece of toast, his seventh of the morning, and wondering whether he could fit in an eighth before leaving the table. "They want to know whether I can float too."

"You see?" said Eleanor triumphantly, pleased that one of her predictions had come true, even if it meant bother for her elder son. "Are they bullying you?"

"Of course not," he replied. "I mean, have you seen me?" He had a point. Henry was fifteen years old by now and played a lot of sports. It was unlikely that any of his classmates would think of picking on him. Even all that marmalade couldn't break through so much muscle. "And, anyway, what do I care if they think I float like Barnaby? It doesn't matter what other people think."

"It matters an enormous amount," said Alistair, putting his coffee down with an exasperated sigh as he picked up Barnaby's dropped copy of *A Tale of Two Cities* and handed it back up to him. "Why, you wouldn't want people to go around saying that you were a—I don't know . . . a piece of Swiss cheese, would you? Or an ornamental teapot? When it wasn't true?"

Melanie sniggered. The idea of her elder brother as either a piece of Swiss cheese or an ornamental teapot was one that clearly tickled her. Even Captain W. E. Johns barked in delight, rolling over on his back and kicking his legs in the air triumphantly.

"They can say what they like about me," said Henry, ignoring them both. "Sticks and stones and all that garbage."

"Are you actually telling me," began Alistair, leaning forward and staring at his elder son as if he barely knew him. "Are you actually telling me that having all your friends know this terrible thing about your brother is not a source of embarrassment to you?"

Henry thought about it for a moment. "Yes," he said, nodding his head. "That's what I'm telling you."

"Even though most of them probably think that you're just a repressed floating boy yourself?"

"Maybe I am," said Henry with a shrug. "I've never felt any great urge to float, but who knows, if the mood took me, under the right circumstances—"

"Henry, are you deliberately trying to upset me?" asked Eleanor, putting her coffee down in exhaustion.

"I'm only telling the truth," said Henry. "It doesn't matter to me that Barnaby floats. It never has mattered. Good luck to him, that's what I say."

"Same goes for me," said Melanie, looking at her elder brother with a sense of pride; Henry could be terribly annoying sometimes, but good Lord, that boy had a heart of gold and wasn't afraid to show it.

"I'd better go to work," said Alistair, standing up and looking at his children in despair. "Sometimes I wonder where I went wrong, do you know that? Where we both went wrong, Eleanor." He leaned over, kissed his wife on the cheek, and they stared at each other meaningfully. "You're sure you don't want me with you today?" he asked quietly.

"I think it will be easier on my own," she replied, looking down into the dregs of her coffee cup.

"All right, then."

"What will be easier on your own?" asked Melanie.

"Nothing," said Alistair, reaching for his briefcase. "I'll see you all tonight." He looked up at Barnaby and hesitated, unable to look the boy fully in the eye. "You'll be all right," he said before turning away and leaving for work, his head bowed low as if a part of him knew that he had committed a most shameful act of cruelty.

"I think I could probably go back to school today," said Barnaby when Henry and Melanie left a few minutes later and Captain W. E. Johns was chasing a squirrel that had had the temerity to stop for a breather in their garden. (It was his intention to put manners on that squirrel.) "I don't want to spend the entire day on the ceiling."

"I thought we might go for a walk," replied Eleanor. "It's such a beautiful day, after all, and neither of us has left the house in more than a week. What do you think—doesn't that sound like a good idea?"

"You're not going to put me on a leash, are you?" asked Barnaby.

"It's your choice," said Eleanor. "The leash or the sandbags."

Barnaby thought about it. "I'll take the sandbags," he said.

The sky was perfectly blue and clear as Eleanor, Barnaby, and Captain W. E. Johns left the house together, the latter having a good nose in all the bushes and hedgerows they passed in case any strange dogs had gone by in the night and left their scent as a deliberate provocation. They made their way south toward the apartments that overlooked the harbor before heading in the direction of the bridge. Barnaby looked up toward the two flags at its northernmost point—the flag of the Australians and the flag of the Aborigines—and found it hard to believe that just over a week before, he had been standing directly beneath them. He could see a line of tiny figures making their way up the side in their blue-and-gray jumpsuits and wondered whether or not Daz was guiding this particular group to the top.

"We're not going back up the bridge, are we?" he asked, and Eleanor shook her head.

"Goodness me, no," she said. "I think we've had quite enough trouble with that bridge for one lifetime, don't you? It's a menace. They should take it down."

"But then how would people get from one side of Sydney to the other?"

"They managed for a hundred years before it was built," said Eleanor. "I'm sure they'd find a way."

Barnaby was already starting to feel a little tired, as it had been nine days since he'd last worn his sandbag rucksack and it was weighing heavily on his shoulders. And his ears were hurting again, the way they did whenever he was forced to stay on the ground.

"Well, if we're not climbing it, where are we going?" he asked as they ascended the steps on the left-hand side onto the long pedestrian walkway that stretched across the water.

"Just for a little exercise, that's all," replied Eleanor. "We'll take a turn around the Opera House and head into the Botanic Gardens. Do you know, I haven't set foot in there in years. Your father used to take me there all the time when we were young and didn't have the problems we have today."

Barnaby, who knew that he was at the top of that particular list, said nothing to this and simply stared into the harbor as they walked, wishing he'd brought a bottle of water with him to quench his thirst. When they had almost reached the other side, Eleanor stopped and knelt to tie one of her laces and Barnaby turned to his left, looking down at the umbrellas over the tables on the rooftop terrace of the Glenmore Hotel, imagining what it would be like to sit there with his family over lunch without having to float on the underside of the canopy. But as Eleanor stood up again, there was a clanging sound of something heavy dropping out of her pocket onto the steel walkway below, and she quickly reached down to retrieve it.

"What was that?" asked Barnaby, turning back and seeing the glint of something metallic in her hands.

"Silly me," she said, showing him the pair of sharp kitchen scissors that she had been carrying in her pocket since they left the house. "I was using these earlier and must have forgotten to put them back in the drawer."

"That's dangerous," said Barnaby.

"Yes, I know. But don't worry, I'll be careful with them."

"Bark," barked Captain W. E. Johns, who knew when something fishy was afoot. "Bark bark bark!"

"Oh, do be quiet," said Eleanor, tugging at his lead.

Descending the staircase into The Rocks, they made their way through the early-morning coffee drinkers before descending another, steeper staircase toward Circular Quay, stopping briefly when Barnaby wanted to listen to an elderly Aborigine man playing the didgeridoo in front of the wharf entrances.

"Come along, Barnaby," said Eleanor irritably.

"I want to hear him play."

"We don't have time. Come along, please."

Barnaby sighed and turned away just as the man finished blowing, and they looked at each other without exchanging a word, leaving the boy feeling rather unsettled. There was something not quite right about today.

When they reached the front of the Opera House, they stopped for a moment to watch the tourists running up and down the steps taking photographs. Barnaby had always been fascinated by the building's design. It reminded him of a ship setting forth on the ocean. "How many operas have you been to there?" he asked.

"Oh, none," said Eleanor. "No one goes to the opera anymore. It's not normal. If I feel like a bit of culture, I turn on *MasterChef* like normal people. Now come along, let's keep walking."

They followed the path round and entered the Botanic Gardens through one of the great iron gates. There weren't many people there, just a few mothers with young babies in their strollers. An ice cream van stood in the corner and a young girl sat in the window, engrossed in a book and looking up occasionally in search of customers.

"Perfect," said Eleanor, appearing pleased by how quiet it was.

"I'm getting tired," said Barnaby. "Can't we stop for a while?"

"Not just yet," replied Eleanor. "A nice walk around the cove and then we can take a break, I promise."

They joined up with a path running through the center of the gardens, and Barnaby looked across at Woolloomooloo Bay, the water sparkling in the morning light, sending a rainbow of color splashing along the surface like a coin skimming across the tops of the waves. There were a few yachts already taking to the water; he could see families on board, mothers and fathers together with their children, all enjoying a happy morning. It was just like it was at the Glenmore. Families together, happy. No one embarrassed by their children.

"Is it much farther?" he asked after another ten

minutes had passed, but Eleanor said nothing, simply continued with all the purpose and suppressed rage of a power-walker.

"We can stop now," she said finally as Barnaby collapsed onto a large rock with a seating platform while Captain W. E. Johns fell at his feet with a dramatic grunt and began to pant loudly. "We're here."

"Where?" asked Barnaby, looking around.

"Mrs. Macquarie's Chair," said Eleanor. "You've read about it in school, haven't you?"

"No."

"Astonishing," she said with a sigh. "What do they teach you children these days anyway? It's part of your history."

Barnaby shrugged. "Maybe I was sick that day," he suggested. "Or being kept off."

"There's always an excuse," said Eleanor. "Well, if that teacher of yours was any good at his job, he'd be bringing you on day-trips to places like this, not dragging you up and down bridges just to get your face in the papers. This is where everything started for Australia. Right here. This is where we all come from." She looked out to sea and breathed in deeply, as if there might be some memories of the lives and times gone by in the flowing scents of the distant Pacific Ocean. "Two hundred years ago," she explained, "Lachlan Macquarie, the governor of New South Wales, lived near here. His wife, Elizabeth, liked to wander down to this very point every morning to watch the ships arrive from England. She would sit here, exactly where you're sitting right now on that rock, and just watch them, day after day. They named this place after her. They called it Mrs. Macquarie's Chair."

Barnaby stood up and looked behind him, worried that he might have stolen a ghost's seat.

"They used to ship the convicts here from England," continued Eleanor. "You know all about that, don't you?"

"Oh yes," said Barnaby, who had learned this much at least in history class.

"And those ships didn't just contain men and women, you know. There were children sent here too. Some of them quite young. As young as you, in fact. They arrived after a long voyage across the ocean to start a new life here in Australia. They didn't know what was in store for them, but they made the best of things and they made it work."

Barnaby tried to imagine what it must have been like for an eight-year-old boy like him to wake up on a ship one morning and see Sydney Harbour coming into view, not knowing what type of life he might end up living on this new continent.

"Even though it seemed frightening at first," Eleanor said, coming toward Barnaby now, "in time they realized that everything that had happened had been for a reason. It is possible, you know, to drift off to an unknown world and find happiness there. Maybe even more happiness than you've ever known before."

Barnaby looked out to sea but said nothing. He felt a rumbling in his stomach and was about to ask Eleanor whether they could get some ice creams from the van at the corner of the park when he heard an unexpected ripping sound and then the start of a *sssss* noise, like a snake might make when it's getting ready to attack.

The ripping sound came from Eleanor's scissors as they cut a hole in the base of his sandbag rucksack.

The *sssss* noise came from the sand that was starting to pour slowly out and form a pyramid on the ground below.

Barnaby looked down in confusion, then back up at his mother, who was shaking her head, unable to look him in the eye.

"I'm sorry, Barnaby," she said. "But it's for the best. There's a wonderful world out there. You can be like one of those early settlers. You'll find happiness somewhere, I'm sure you will."

Barnaby gasped as the sand continued to empty—he was like a human egg timer—and Captain W. E. Johns bounded over and stuck his nose in it for a moment before looking up at his master in panic as the boy's feet started to lift a little off the ground.

the terrible thing

"Mum!" he cried. "Mum! Help! I'm going up! Captain W. E. Johns, help me!"

"I'm sorry, Barnaby," Eleanor repeated, her voice catching a little now. "Truly I am."

Captain W. E. Johns barked and started to run around in circles, then leaped in the air as Barnaby continued to rise, trying to grab hold of one of his feet with his mouth, but it was too late—the sand had almost run out and Barnaby was rising higher and higher into the sky.

"Mum!" he cried one last time as he reached the height of the trees. "Help me! I'm sorry! I'll try not to float anymore!"

"It's too late, Barnaby," she cried, waving up at him, bidding him goodbye. "Look after yourself!"

And a minute later he had risen too high to make his voice heard anymore. His mother, his dog, and the magnificent city of Sydney were disappearing beneath him, and with no mattress to stop him from going any farther, Barnaby Brocket simply continued to rise, unsure what was going to happen to him next.

Chapter 7

Approaching from a Northwesterly Direction

Barnaby closed his eyes, as he didn't want to watch the ground disappearing beneath him any longer. He didn't suffer from vertigo in the way that Stephen Hebden did, but still, the higher he rose, the more frightened he became.

When he finally dared to open them again, a flock of galahs had gathered beside him and were hovering there, staring with impatient expressions on their faces, unhappy that their airspace was being invaded by an eight-year-old boy. They pecked him a little, flapping their feathers in his face, but flew on a few minutes later, leaving Barnaby to rise higher in the sky. He glanced to his left and was pleased to see something—another creature perhaps—approaching in the distance, a little higher in the sky but making its way toward him. He watched and soon realized that it wasn't a creature at all but a basket with a large balloon hooked above it and a great flame keeping the whole thing aloft.

on the coming wind

“Help!” cried Barnaby, waving his arms in the air, which only made him ascend even faster. “I’m over here.”

The hot-air balloon continued to approach from a northwesterly direction, and it soon became clear that if Barnaby timed things accurately, he could position himself underneath it at precisely the moment it reached him. He flapped his arms and kicked his feet, like a deep-sea diver making his way to the surface of the ocean, before slowing down a little, keeping both eyes fixed firmly on the balloon.

A few minutes later it was almost directly above him and Barnaby flapped again until he ascended another few feet, banging his head against the underside of the basket.

“Ow,” said Barnaby Brocket.

“Who’s down there?” came a voice from within—a female voice of a certain age.

“Help me, please,” cried Barnaby. “Can you pull me into your basket?”

“Heavens above!” said another voice—another female voice of the same certain age. “It’s a little boy. Ethel, fetch me the fishing net.”

A strong silver pole with a threaded hoop at the end emerged from the balloon and scooped Barnaby up, pulling him through the air and depositing him on the floor of the basket, and he started to float up toward the flames.

"Please," he cried. "Tie me to the side. Otherwise, I'm going to be burned alive."

"Heavens above!" said the two women in unison, grabbing him by both arms and doing exactly as he'd asked. Once he was safely secured, they stared down at him with a mixture of amazement and recognition.

"I know you," said the first woman, whose name was Marjorie, pointing a wrinkled finger at his nose. "I saw you on the news last week. You were the millionth person to climb the Sydney Harbour Bridge."

"The ten millionth, actually," said Barnaby.

"Who is he?" asked Ethel. The women both had hairstyles that resembled crow's nests, and a collection of knitting needles and chopsticks held the entire mess together. "Who did you say he was, Marjorie?"

"You remember, dear. We saw him on the television the evening we arrived. He climbed the bridge with his school friends and set some sort of record. Everyone got terribly excited. Then it turned out that he kept floating away. It was a very odd business."

"Oh, *that* boy," replied Ethel, peering down at Barnaby. "Was that really you?"

"Yes, that was me," he admitted.

"But what are you doing up here? It's not often we have to pull people into our balloon, you know. In fact, it's the first time."

"The second, Ethel," said Marjorie. "You remember the human cannonball over Barcelona?"

"Oh yes, of course. But then he rather fell into our basket, didn't he? We didn't have to scoop him up."

Barnaby opened his mouth but was reluctant to get his mother into trouble. "It's my own fault, really," he said. "I forgot my sandbags, and before I knew it, I was up in the air."

"Sandbags?" asked Ethel, frowning.

"They keep my feet on the ground."

"Well, no good ever came of that."

"There's not much we can do about it now anyway," said Marjorie. "I hope you don't think that we can take you back to Sydney? Here you are and here you have to stay."

"But I need to go home," said Barnaby.

"Can't be done, I'm afraid, even if we wanted to. It's the winds, you see. They don't blow us back in that direction. We have to go east. Lucky for you the world is round, eh? If this was the fourteenth century, then the world would still be flat and we'd all fall off the edge."

Barnaby frowned as he tried to make sense of this. Behind him, perhaps only a few miles away, were the northern suburbs and the house where his parents, brother, sister, and dog lived. He surely wasn't going to have to go all the way around the world to see them again, was he?

"He's being dishonest," said Ethel, leaning forward and looking him directly in the eye. "Marjorie, I tell you he's being dishonest. All little boys lie, that's a scientific fact, but this one is easy to read. I can see it in his eyes. Tell the truth, boy. What are you really doing up here?"

Barnaby was about to proclaim his innocence, but something about these two ladies suggested to him that they wouldn't let him alone until he came clean, and so he decided to tell the full story, warts and all.

"But that's outrageous," said Ethel when he was finished.

"Shocking!" agreed Marjorie. "What kind of mother would do that to her child?"

"You know very well what type of mother, Marjorie," said Ethel sadly.

"As do you, Ethel," said Marjorie, in an equally sorrowful voice.

"And by the sound of things, the father was in on it too."

"Absolutely disgraceful."

"And you want to go back to them, do you?" Ethel asked, looking at Barnaby as if she couldn't quite believe that he would consider going home. "Even after they set you adrift like this?"

Barnaby thought about it. Until this moment he hadn't given any thought to the question of whether or not he wanted to go back—it just seemed like the most obvious thing to do. He was only eight years old, after all. Where would he live if he didn't go home? What would he eat? How would he survive?

"You don't have to worry about any of those things," said Ethel, reading his mind as easily as she had seen through his earlier story. "You can come with us. Ever been to South America?"

"No," said Barnaby, shaking his head. "I've never been outside Sydney."

"Then you have a real treat in store for you. We're heading home to Brazil. We have a coffee farm there, you see. We've been on holiday for a few months, but it's time to get back. That's where we were going when you bumped into us. It won't take long. She's a wonderful balloon, isn't she, Marjorie?"

"Wonderful, Ethel. The best we've ever had."

"Bar none."

"Bar absolutely none."

Barnaby struggled to his feet, making sure to keep his arms within the ropes, and looked over the side of the balloon. The land had vanished now and he found himself staring at a group of wispy white clouds as they floated past.

"What do you think?" asked Ethel. "Are you ready for an adventure?"

"I don't really have much choice, do I?" he asked.

"Splendid! Then full steam ahead."

"Full *flame,* Marjorie, dear."

"Of course, Ethel, dear."

A little later, once their coordinates were fully established and their navigation charts folded correctly, they opened a picnic basket and offered Barnaby a sandwich, an apple, and a flask of orange juice.

"So what's in South America?" he asked as he ate. "Do your husbands live there?"

"Husbands?" cried Ethel, looking at Marjorie in horror.

"Husbands?" roared Marjorie, staring at Ethel as if someone had just threatened to sit on her head.

"We don't have husbands, young man," explained Ethel. "Nasty, smelly creatures. Always lazing around like the good-for-nothings they are. Drinking, gambling on horses, finding excuses not to fix the crooked shelf in the kitchen. Making the most foul noises and disgusting stenches from unspeakable parts of their horrible bodies while they're sitting watching *sport* on the television."

"Sport!" repeated Marjorie with a shudder.

"No, we gave up on the idea of husbands many years ago. Never had any interest in them, did we, Marjorie?"

"Not even the faintest inclination, Ethel."

"Have you been friends for a long time, then?" asked Barnaby.

"Oh yes," said Marjorie. "Since we were in our early twenties, which is more than forty years ago now, if you can believe it. We met when we both joined an amateur dramatic society in Shropshire, took one look at each other, and decided that we were destined to be—"

"Friends," interrupted Ethel, patting Marjorie gently on the hand and smiling at her. "The very *best* of friends."

"The very *closest* of friends," agreed Marjorie.

"Exactly," said Ethel, nodding her head with a sigh of deep satisfaction. "Nothing wrong with that, is there?"

"No, of course not," said Barnaby. "I had a very good friend once called Liam McGonagall. He saved my life when the school we were in burned to the ground. Well, I say *school,* but it was more like a prison."

"Did *you* burn it down?" asked Marjorie, leaning forward again and poking him with one of her chopsticks.

"No," said Barnaby. "I wouldn't do something like that."

"You won't be getting any ideas with that flame up there, will you?"

"I didn't burn it down!" insisted Barnaby. "The place was a firetrap."

"I thought maybe that was why your mother sent you away."

"She sent me away because she said I wasn't normal."

For the first time, both ladies were silent; they stared at Barnaby, then at each other, before looking back at the boy.

"Do you know," said Ethel, more quietly now, "forty years ago my mother told me that I wasn't normal either and threw me out of the house. I never saw her again. She wouldn't take my calls, refused to reply to any of my letters. It was a terrible thing."

"My father said much the same thing to me," added Marjorie. "Closed the door in my face forever."

"But I don't understand," said Barnaby. "You seem perfectly normal to me. You don't look any different from the old ladies who live on our street."

"Less of the old, you little brat, or we'll toss you overboard," said Marjorie, glaring at him but then bursting into an extraordinary laugh, her whole body shaking, as if someone was tickling her all over.

"Don't, Marjorie," said Ethel, giggling too. "The poor boy will think you're serious."

"Oh, nonsense!" insisted Marjorie. "I haven't been serious since nineteen eighty-two. I wouldn't throw you overboard, young man. Don't worry."

"Thank you," said Barnaby, relieved.

"Anyway, the point is, just because your version

of normal isn't the same as someone else's version doesn't mean that there's anything wrong with you."

"Quite right, Marjorie," said Ethel, nodding fiercely. "If I'd listened to my mother when she said there was something wrong with me, I'd have lived a very lonely life."

"And if I'd listened to my father, I'd have been miserable."

"Who wants to be normal anyway?" cried Ethel, throwing her arms in the air. "I know I don't."

"But if I had been normal, then my parents wouldn't have sent me away," said Barnaby. "I'd still be at home with Henry, Melanie, and Captain W. E. Johns."

"What are they—cats?"

"Henry's my elder brother," explained Barnaby. "And Melanie's my elder sister."

"And Captain W. E. Johns?"

"My dog."

"Breed?"

"Indeterminate."

"Parentage?"

"Unknown."

Neither Ethel nor Marjorie had any answer to this so they said nothing, simply shook their heads and continued to steer the hot-air balloon in the general direction of South America.

"You should get some rest," said Ethel after a few

minutes. "It's a long way to Brazil. Do you want to steer, Marjorie, or shall I?"

And anxious to prove himself agreeable, Barnaby Brocket curled up in a corner of the basket, closed his eyes, and within a minute or two was sound asleep.

Chapter 8

The Coffee Farm

When Barnaby woke, he was surprised to find himself lying in a comfortable bed with a warm blanket spread across his body, two fluffy pillows under his head, and a garden hose wrapped around the entire thing to keep him from rising to the ceiling, where a fan with four rotary blades was threatening to turn him into mincemeat. He sat up carefully, held on to the sheets, and looked out of the window.

A vast farm stretched before him, rows and rows of tall green plants and a dozen or more people walking between the stalks, each wearing a pair of pale blue dungarees and a wide-brimmed hat to ward off the sun. As they examined the stems, they shouted at each other and made extravagant hand gestures, sniffing a few of the leaves, pleased by some, uncertain about others. Clumps of small red berries sprouted from each vine, and from time to time one of the workers would twist one off before tossing it into his mouth and chewing thoughtfully, forehead creased in concentration as he considered the taste, before spitting the mess into the dirt at his feet.

Barnaby couldn't believe that he had slept through the balloon landing and the journey to the farm, and was beginning to feel a little uncertain of where exactly he was when the door was flung open and the two ladies charged into the room.

"He's awake, Ethel," said Marjorie.

"About time too. How long has it been anyway?"

"Almost thirty-six hours."

"I've been asleep for thirty-six hours?" asked Barnaby, opening his eyes wide in surprise. "Are you sure?"

"Oh, quite sure," said Ethel. "There was no waking you, despite the fact that we came down with an almighty thud. Which, by the way, accounts for that bump on your forehead, in case you're wondering."

Barnaby reached up and felt a tenderness just above his right eye. "Ow," he said.

"Well, floating up into the sky will take it out of you, so it's no wonder you were tired," said Marjorie. "When we landed, we thought we'd better bring you here until you decide what you want to do next. We put you in Vincente's old room. He wasn't much older than you when he first came to live with us, and he was always so happy in here. He said it was the most comfortable bed he'd ever slept in."

"Well, it was the *only* bed he'd ever slept in," said Ethel. "So there wasn't much competition."

"Who's Vincente?" asked Barnaby.

"He's a boy we looked after for a while, but he lives in America now," replied Marjorie. "A wonderful young man. Such a delight to have around. We miss him terribly. Anyway, what would you like to do today?"

"I want to go home," said Barnaby.

"Yes, of course. But Australia is very far away, that's the problem. It's not easy to get there from Brazil."

"But we did a little research," said Marjorie, a triumphant smile spreading across her face. "And it turns out you can fly to Sydney direct from Rio de Janeiro. Well, there's a stopover in Hong Kong, but it's only for a few hours."

"It's a long flight, though," added Ethel. "Do you think you can manage it?"

"I'll have to," said Barnaby, pleased to think that he would have a trip in an aeroplane to add to his hot-air balloon journey. "Is the airport far from here?"

"A few hundred miles. You'll need to take a train. The Fonseca Express goes from São Paulo, where we are now, to New York, but it stops off in Rio along the way. You're not in a hurry, though, are you?"

"Well, not a terrible hurry, I suppose," said Barnaby.

"Good. Because we've checked with the airline and there isn't a seat available until the end of the week. You can stay here in the meantime if you like."

Barnaby nodded. The two ladies were being kind enough to offer him not only a ticket back to Australia but free room and board; the least he could do was appear grateful.

"Good, well, that's all settled, then. You'll stay here until Saturday, then off you go home. We might even have a little party in your honor before you leave. In the meantime, you might as well enjoy your time here. Do you know much about Brazil?"

"Nothing at all," said Barnaby, shaking his head. "We haven't studied South America in geography class yet."

"I've always said that young people should know as much about foreign countries as they possibly can," said Marjorie, nodding her head wisely. "Just in case they get thrown out of home."

"Or run away," said Ethel.

"Or *float* away," said Marjorie, smiling at her, and Ethel burst out laughing and they jumped in the air and high-fived each other, which was something that Barnaby had never seen two elderly ladies do before. "Of course, we didn't know anything at all about Brazil when we first got here," she added. "But once our families decided they didn't want anything to do with us, we wanted to get as far away from them as possible."

"And we both liked coffee," said Ethel.

"*Loved* coffee," corrected Marjorie.

"So we thought what fun it would be to start our own coffee farm."

"Here in Brazil."

"On this very plantation."

"And we've been here for—oh, how long has it been now, Ethel?"

"Almost forty years."

"Has it really been that long?"

"It has, yes."

"It's hard to believe, isn't it?"

"Well, we've been so very happy," replied Ethel, and the two ladies smiled at each other and had a little hug. Barnaby noticed that they were holding hands, which was another curious thing, but they seemed to be doing it without even noticing. He couldn't remember the last time he'd seen his father and mother holding hands. In fact, Alistair had always said that people who showed any affection toward each other in public were just looking for attention, nothing more.

"Oh dear," said Marjorie, dabbing at her eyes with a handkerchief. "Have I got something in my eye, Ethel?"

"Let me have a look, dear. Oh yes, you do. Just a moment. Hold still now."

"Oh, be careful—you know how I hate people touching my eyes."

"Don't be such a goose. There, it's all gone. Better?"

"Much better, thank you. You're a lifesaver. Now, Barnaby, you must be hungry. Would you like some breakfast?"

A short time later, Barnaby was seated in the kitchen with an extraordinary amount of food spread out before him. There were eggs cooked in every possible way, sausages, strips of bacon and piles of hash browns, bowls filled with chilies and peppers, plates overflowing with roasted mushrooms and fried onions. Pitchers of orange juice and ice-cold water stood in the center of the table, and as Barnaby ate—a mosquito net thrown over his body and pinned to the floor, the top cut away for his head to poke through—he watched the farmworkers as they drifted in and out, attending to their business. They all seemed delighted to see the two ladies and greeted them with hugs and kisses.

"Oh, Thiago, get off me, you disgusting creature," cried Ethel, giggling a little as a rather fat man with a heavy, dark mustache threw his arms around her and squeezed her to within an inch of her life. His shirt was open halfway down his stomach; it was not a pleasant sight.

"Ah, Miss Ethel," he said, smiling in such a way that, just as his eyebrows pointed downward, the ends of his mustache stretched upward, so the two almost met. "It hasn't been the same here without you. You must never leave us again." He wagged a finger in the air, and his tone became half mocking, half serious. "The trouble there has been since you went away."

"Now, you know perfectly well that every so often Marjorie and I need a break," said Ethel. "We'd go mad if we didn't take one of our ballooning holidays. But, yes, I have heard about what's been going on, and I'm very angry with you, Thiago. Very angry indeed. I would have expected a little more kindness and understanding on your part."

Barnaby frowned. For someone who was very angry, very angry indeed, Ethel did not sound annoyed, although she did sound a little disappointed.

"Ah," said Thiago, shaking his head and turning away, his face showing a mixed expression of sorrow and pain. "We will not talk of it now. But I see you brought a little surprise home with you." He walked over to Barnaby and looked him up and down. "Who is this?"

"This is Barnaby Brocket," said Marjorie. "He's staying with us for the rest of the week. He's trying to get home to Australia."

"He's inside a mosquito net."

"He floats," she explained. "The poor boy can't keep his feet on the ground for more than a couple of seconds."

Thiago chewed on the inside of his lips as he thought about this, then threw his arms in the air as if to suggest that it took all sorts to make a world.

"You like to pick coffee beans, Barnaby?" asked Thiago.

"I've never done it."

"You like football?"

"Yes, but only to watch. If I try to play, I float away."

"Hmm. Well, what *do* you like to do, then?"

Barnaby thought about it. "I like to read," he said. "I like books."

"Oh dear," said Marjorie, looking a little embarrassed. "I don't think we have any books in the house. Not English-language ones anyway. They're all in Portuguese. Can you read Portuguese?"

"No," said Barnaby, shaking his head.

"Then I don't think we have anything for you, I'm afraid."

Just as she said this, a young girl of about eighteen came into the kitchen carrying a basket filled to the brim with laundry. She stopped in her tracks when she saw the four people gathered there. And then the most extraordinary thing happened. Thiago, staring at her with an expression of fury on his face, reached across to the table, picked up Barnaby's empty plate, and threw it on the floor, smashing it into a dozen or more pieces, before marching back outside.

"Well, that wasn't necessary, surely," said Marjorie, shaking her head as she reached for a dustpan and brush.

"You poor dear," said Ethel, walking over to the girl and putting an arm around her. "And you shouldn't be carrying all this laundry anyway. Not in your condition." She took the basket and placed it on the counter. "Barnaby," she said, turning round. "This is Palmira, who has lived with us since she was a little girl. Thiago, the gentleman who just left, is her father. He's a little out of sorts at the moment, as you can probably tell."

Barnaby wasn't sure what to say—he'd never seen such bizarre behavior—but found that he couldn't keep his eyes off Palmira, who had quite the most beautiful face he had ever seen.

"Don't worry, dear," said Marjorie, patting Palmira on the shoulder. "He'll come round. He just needs time, that's all."

The girl shook her head, her face filled with sorrow, before picking up the laundry basket again and leaving the room. Barnaby's eyes followed her, and he was aware of a strange pang in his stomach that he'd never experienced before. For the first time in his life, he felt as if he was floating up to the ceiling, even though his feet were firmly on the floor.

Chapter 9

Something to Read at Last

A few days later, Barnaby was sitting on his own in one of the barns, holding a sack of coffee beans on his lap to stop himself from floating away, when Palmira came in with a glass of ice-cold orange juice and a sandwich.

"I'm sorry," she said, pausing in the doorway. "I didn't know you were in here."

"It's all right," said Barnaby, who had been feeling a little lonely anyway and was glad of some company. "You can join me if you like."

Palmira smiled and sat beside him on one of the overturned barrels. "I usually take my breaks out here," she said. "It's quiet. I can be alone with my thoughts."

Barnaby nodded. He wondered whether she wanted to be on her own now, but he didn't want to pass up the opportunity to spend some time with her. The night before, he'd had a dream about Palmira in which they'd decided to go back to

Sydney together; a part of him wanted to tell her about it but he was too embarrassed.

"You like it here at the farm?" she asked him.

"Very much," said Barnaby. "Ethel and Marjorie have been very kind to me."

"They are good people," she agreed. "My father and I are very grateful to them."

"I like Thiago," said Barnaby. "He taught me how to ride a donkey."

Barnaby thought he could see tears forming in Palmira's eyes when he said this. She placed a hand on her stomach for a moment and held it there, and he wondered whether she was feeling sick. "He has taught me many things too," she said. "But now he will not even speak to me."

"Were you born here?" asked Barnaby, and Palmira shook her head.

"Not here," she said. "Not even in Brazil. My family were very poor. I was born in Argentina, in a city that knew nothing but poverty. My mother died when I was a baby, and soon after this my father and I moved across the border and found this coffee farm. Miss Ethel and Miss Marjorie took us in, and we've been here ever since."

"Did you know Vincente?" asked Barnaby, who had discovered in his bedroom a set of sketchbooks filled with the most extraordinary drawings, each one signed with that name. Most of them were of people, but they weren't quite like any people that

Barnaby had seen before. The figures stood in the center of the pages, but they were surrounded by things that seemed to be part of the subject's life. Not things they owned, but things they felt. One drawing that he particularly liked featured a young boy of about Barnaby's age, and all around him were colors and thunderbolts, empty plates, and intricate maps of South America. When he turned it over, he found the words *Self-Portrait* written in a neat hand on the other side.

"Yes, of course," replied Palmira. "He lived here all through his youth."

"Can you tell me anything about him? I've been looking at all the work he left behind. I've never seen anything like it. And that enormous painting in the hallway next to the kitchen—that's one of his, right?"

"Yes. It's beautiful, isn't it? I could stare at it for hours. Miss Ethel and Miss Marjorie met him when he was only eight or nine years old. They found him creating . . . What is the word? Drawings and paintings on the side of a building?"

"Art?" suggested Barnaby.

"Graffiti," said Palmira. "At that time, he was drawing insulting pictures of our president, who was a son of a dog and stole the wealth of the people in order to build golden bathtubs in his palace and bathe in the sweat of the working man."

"Gross," said Barnaby, pulling a face.

"It's a metaphor," said Palmira with a shrug. "The whole country despised this man, but we lived in fear of him too. He had the army under his control and could not be removed. He taxed us beyond our means and didn't care whether we had enough money to feed ourselves. The newspapers were afraid to criticize him for fear they might be closed down and their editors thrown into the streets. The writers had no courage either. Only this little boy, still a child, discovered a way to express the people's dissatisfaction with his rule. And with paint that he found who knows where—in the slum heaps, in the dustbins, in the trash piles—he created magnificent pictures on the walls of the city, full of strange colors and curious designs, which showed the world who this man was at his heart. The people became enamored of him, and the police wanted to hunt him down and capture him. If they had discovered his whereabouts, he would have been sent to jail, maybe even to his death, but one night Miss Ethel and Miss Marjorie happened upon him when they were in the city and followed him back to his slum—only to find that he lived alone in a little corner on a pile of cardboard boxes."

"Where were his parents?" asked Barnaby.

"Vanished," replied Palmira. "So they took Vincente back to the coffee farm and brought him up as if he was their own son. They educated him, gave him clean canvases and expensive paints and brushes, encouraged his talent to grow more and more every day. Finally, he became a great painter and left for New York, where he soon became one of the most famous and celebrated artists in the land. And he owes it all to those two ladies."

"There seem to be a lot of people here without families," said Barnaby. "Ethel and Marjorie told me that they were sent away from their families too. Because they were different. But they seem perfectly normal to me."

Palmira smiled. "That's because they are," she said. "We all are. Their idea of normal just happens to be different from some other people's idea of normal. But this is the world we live in. Some people simply cannot accept something that is outside of their experience."

"My mother had never known anyone who floated before," said Barnaby. "I think that's why she cut a hole in my rucksack." He thought about it and bowed his head a little. "Maybe she just didn't love me," he said. "Not the way I am."

"A mother will always love her child," said Palmira, putting an arm around him and pulling him close. "No matter what he does or who he is. I know this for certain. I know it already."

Barnaby cuddled up closer to Palmira and said nothing more, feeling very sad that he was here in Brazil with people he barely knew and not in Sydney, throwing a ball around the living room for Captain W. E. Johns. He would have happily stayed in Palmira's embrace for the entire afternoon, only a sound behind them made them both turn round to see Thiago standing on the other side of the barn, listening to their conversation. Perhaps it was the way the sunlight was streaming in through the opposite doors, but Barnaby was sure that his cheeks were wet, as if he had been crying. But he couldn't look for long because the moment they turned round and Thiago realized that he had been discovered, he disappeared out into the coffee farm.

On Friday night, the ladies held a barbecue for Barnaby to wish him well on his journey back to Australia. They gave him two tickets in a colorful envelope, one for the train to Rio de Janeiro, the other for the plane back to Sydney, and later, when he went to thank them for their many kindnesses, he found them talking to one of the women who worked on the farm.

"And Palmira hasn't heard from him since he left?" Marjorie was saying, and Barnaby frowned, wondering who they were talking about.

"Not a word. There's more chance of the Stone Age returning than there is of that boy coming back to São Paulo," said the woman, whose name was Maria-Consuela. "There's more chance of dinosaurs ruling the Earth once again! We all knew he was bad news from the start. I said it and you both heard me. I took one look at that pretty face and said he was the devil incarnate! *El diablo!* And I promise you that if Thiago ever catches up with him, there will be trouble like there has never been before."

"Well, if that brutish boy is gone, then good riddance to him," said Ethel. "I only wish Thiago would take care of Palmira again. He's lost without her, anyone can see that. And she needs her father now more than ever before. It seems to me that if— Oh, Barnaby! Did no one ever tell you that you shouldn't eavesdrop on other people's conversations?"

"I'm sorry," he said quickly. "Only I wanted to thank you for letting me stay here this week."

"You're very welcome," said Ethel. "But are you really sure you want to go? Your parents did such a terrible thing, after all. I don't know why you want to go back there."

"They might be regretting it now," said Barnaby. "If I can just get back to Australia, then I'll know for sure. Thiago bought me a postcard in the village, and I'm going to send it to them tomorrow to tell them I'm on my way."

"I think we should have a toast," said Marjorie, calling all the workers together and raising her glass to Barnaby. "What fun it's been to have you here," she said. "And I think Palmira has a little present for you, don't you, dear?"

The girl stepped forward, a shy smile on her face that made Barnaby's heart skip a beat. "Since you are leaving us, I thought you might like something to remember us by," she said, handing him a beautifully wrapped package. "Something to remember *me* by."

Barnaby smiled in excitement as he took off the paper and was delighted to find a small English-language edition of the *Adventures of Sherlock Holmes* inside. He hadn't read anything in a week and was worried that his imagination was going to close down for good.

"Thank you!" he said, rushing forward and giving her a hug. "But where did you find it? I thought there were no English books here."

"I have my ways," she said, winking at him. Seeing how much pleasure she had given the boy with a single book made everyone at the barbecue burst into a round of applause, and Palmira smiled at them, gazing around in happiness at this unusual family before locking eyes with the one she loved most of all, her father, Thiago. His face was grim, but then he started to smile, remembering how she had consoled Barnaby when he was upset about his family, and seeing how she had delighted him by offering this thoughtful gift, and his heart broke for the daughter he loved as he ran forward and wrapped his arms around her, holding her close, and whispering words in her ear that made her understand she had a father who would never be separated from her or her baby ever again.

The following day, as Barnaby boarded the Fonseca Express, he could barely keep his eyes open. He had partied long into the night and barely slept at all. Now he found a seat in an empty compartment, put on his seat belt to prevent himself from floating to the ceiling, and kicked his shoes off, yawning loudly, and hoping that no one would come in to disturb him. He read "A Scandal in Bohemia," the first of the Sherlock Holmes stories, and barely noticed the time passing. When he finished, he put the book away and wrote the postcard home; when the conductor came to check his ticket, he promised to put it in the station mailbox at the next stop.

And then, without thinking to set an alarm to wake him when the train arrived in Rio de Janeiro, Barnaby closed his eyes and fell asleep.

Dear Family.

You're probably wondering where I am since I haven't been home in more than a week. After I floated away, I got saved by two ladies in a hot air baloon, but because of the direction of the winds I wasn't able to come straight home. You can't turn a baloon around, you see. You have to go the way the WIND BLOWS. And it blew me all the way to BRAZIL.

I miss Sydney and all of you.

I'm on my way home and will see you soon. I'll try not to float anymore but I'm not sure how. But I Promise to do my best.

A special hello to Captain W.E. Johns,

Your Son / brother / master,

Barnaby

P.S when I come home, I'd like to invite my friend Palmira to visit us. she's never been to Australia, but says she'd like to.

MURPHY BROS. PRESS, INC.

M BP

POST CARD

Brasil 2009 CALENDÁRIO LUNAR CHINÊS - ANO DO BOI R$ 2,35

XXIV Bienal de São Paulo VAN GOGH BRASIL 98 R$ 0,31

Goiânia • GO

TO Mr & Mrs Brocket,
Henry, Melanie
& Captain W.E. Johns

15 Waruda Street
Kirribilli
NSW 2061
AUSTRALia

Chapter 10

The Worst Jeremy Potts Ever

Alistair opened the mailbox and glanced at the bills and junk mail he held in his hand before noticing the postcard squashed between a flyer for a home-cleaning company and a menu for a newly opened pizza delivery service. He recognized the handwriting immediately, and his heart beat a little faster as he started to read it.

In the nine days since Barnaby had floated away, the Brocket household had become a decidedly difficult place to be. Henry and Melanie were causing all sorts of bother, insisting that the police be called to search for their missing brother, but when Alistair told them that both he and their mother might be in serious trouble if the truth came out, they became a little less eager.

"The authorities take a very dim view of these things," he said. "Why, before you know it, we could be up in court and you two could be living in foster homes. And, anyway, it's not as if it's our fault that

Barnaby isn't here anymore. After all, he was the one who took his rucksack off."

This was the official explanation that Alistair and Eleanor had agreed upon. Barnaby had taken the bag off his shoulders, complaining yet again about the weight of the thing, and before he knew it, he was up in the air. Eleanor tried to save him but she couldn't jump high enough. He'd been told a thousand times, they said, how important it was to keep it on, but he was too willful to listen.

Everything that had happened, they insisted, was Barnaby's own fault.

But this was not enough to satisfy Henry and Melanie, who missed their brother dreadfully and were causing scenes in front of their parents every evening, insisting that more be done to find him. Neither of them imagined for a moment that their parents weren't telling the truth. After all, there had been only one witness to the terrible thing that had happened at Mrs. Macquarie's Chair, and that was Captain W. E. Johns.

And it wasn't as if he could expose the lie.

If only the child had been normal, Alistair thought, looking up and down the street at the rows of even hedges and perfectly manicured lawns. Was it too much to ask for a child to fit in? He remembered when he was Barnaby's age. He'd done everything he could not to stand out from the crowd, but it wasn't possible, not with all the attention-seeking that his own parents had insisted upon.

He felt sick to his stomach when he remembered how desperate they had been for everyone to pay attention to their son. His father, Rupert, dreamed of being an actor; his mother, Claudia, of being an actress. They'd met in drama school in their early twenties, when they were quite convinced that they were going to become international film stars.

"I want to work with the very best directors," said Claudia, who had only ever had a small part in a television advertisement for artificially sweetened breakfast cereal, in which she played a spoon.

"And with actors who really respect the craft," added Rupert, who had won the role of "Thug in Café" in an episode of an early-evening soap opera when he was sixteen years old.

Stardom somehow eluded them, though, and so when Alistair was born, they developed a new ambition: to turn their son into a star instead.

From the time he learned to walk, the boy was dragged to auditions for commercials, plays, and television drama series, despite the fact that he had no interest in taking part in such things and would have preferred to stay at home, playing with his friends. A naturally shy boy, he hated standing up in front of complete strangers and having to perform a scene from *Oliver!* or sing a version of "With a Little Bit of Bloomin' Luck" in a ridiculous Cockney accent.

"You'll do it or you won't get any dinner," Claudia told him when he was eleven years old and complaining about being forced to audition for the part of Jeremy Potts in an amateur dramatic production of *Chitty Chitty Bang Bang.*

"But I don't want to be Jeremy Potts," complained Alistair. "I want to be Alistair Brocket."

"And who is Alistair Brocket?" cried Rupert, appalled that his son would allow such a great opportunity to pass him by. "Nobody! Nobody at all! Is that how you want to spend your life? Without anyone paying you any attention? Look at your mother and me—we could have been giants of the film industry, but we gave it all up to become the parents of an ungrateful little boy. And this is the thanks we get."

Alistair said nothing to this. He knew very well that they hadn't given anything up for him—that they'd been trying to be actors for years before he was born, so their lack of success was nothing to do with him.

To his horror, and owing to the dearth of better choices, Alistair won the part. For weeks, he attended rehearsals reluctantly, having great difficulty remembering his lines and always dreading the moment when it was his turn to sing. It was bad enough with just the other cast members and director watching, but whenever he thought of a full audience sitting out there in a darkened auditorium, it was enough to make him want to throw up.

"I don't want to do it," he told his parents the day the play was due to open. "Please don't make me."

But nothing he could say could make them change their minds, and a few hours later he went onstage with his legs feeling like jelly. Over the course of the two hours that followed, at a conservative estimate he remembered less than five percent of his lines, fell off the stage twice, tripped over his co-star's feet six times, and gave every impression of being about to wet his pants when Grandpa Potts declared that up from the ashes, up from the ashes, grow the roses of success.

The local newspaper was scathing in its review, and the next day, in school, he was ridiculed by his classmates.

"Never again," he told his parents when he went home that evening, wishing the ground would open up and swallow him whole. "I'm not going back onstage *ever,* and you can't make me. It's humiliating. I am never, *ever,* going to stand out from the crowd again."

Walking toward his front door now, some thirty years later, Alistair couldn't help but feel anger at his parents for putting him through this trauma at such a young age. Why, if they'd only let him be himself—a quiet, thoughtful, kind child—then maybe he would never have developed such a terrible fear of being noticed in the first place.

And then perhaps he wouldn't have cared so much what people thought of his own children.

"Anything in the post?" asked Eleanor as he went into the kitchen and looked around at his family, who were eating their breakfast. Henry and Melanie said nothing; they were maintaining a silence to show their parents how much they missed Barnaby, but neither Alistair nor Eleanor was giving them the satisfaction of noticing it. He glanced up at the ceiling, from where Barnaby's mattress had been recently removed, and crumpled up the postcard, stuffing it in his pocket, determined to throw it in the wastepaper basket at work later that morning.

"Nothing," he said, betraying a slight catch in his throat as he shook his head. "Nothing except bills and junk mail."

Chapter 11

The Cotton-Swab Prince

"Last stop! Last stop!"

Barnaby opened his eyes and gave a great stretch, unsure exactly where he was at first and then remembering: the Fonseca Express.

"It smells like coffee in here," said the conductor, opening the window to allow the air in.

"It's my rucksack," explained Barnaby, sitting up and unfastening his seat belt before pulling it on, for the bag, filled to the brim with coffee beans, had been a parting gift from Ethel and Marjorie, something to keep him grounded when he arrived in Rio de Janeiro. He'd been so tired when he arrived at the train station in São Paulo, but the journey must have refreshed him, for he felt very alert now, as if he'd slept for days. Stepping down onto the platform, however, he was surprised to see a sign that said PENN STATION.

"Excuse me," he asked a passing policeman. "Which direction do I go for Rio de Janeiro Airport?"

"About five thousand miles that way, kid," the man replied, pointing toward the exit doors.

"Five thousand miles?" said Barnaby, gasping in astonishment. "Where am I exactly?"

"New York," said the cop. "The most magnificent city in the world."

"Actually, that's Sydney," said Barnaby, who might have been surprised to find himself in North America rather than South, but wasn't going to allow a mistake like that to go unchallenged. The policeman didn't seem to mind, however, simply shrugging his shoulders and moving on while Barnaby made his way out of the station, wondering what on earth he should do next. He had obviously slept for the entire journey, and his flight to Sydney had departed without him.

Barnaby was now alone on the streets of the huge city and simply wandered around for an hour, down one avenue, across a side street, up another, through a plaza, and out into a busy shopping area, a little taken aback by the height of the buildings and the crowds that were making their way along the pavements. After a while he saw a long queue forming to get into one of the skyscrapers and looked at the marble sign pinned to the wall: THE CHRYSLER BUILDING. Just then a man pushed into him from behind, pulled the rucksack off his back, and ran off down the street with it.

"Hey!" Barnaby shouted. "Stop, thief!"

But there was nothing he could do. Before he could even think of giving chase, his feet were lifting off the ground and he was rising up into the sky. And as he approached the top of the building, his head banged sharply against a hard metal object, and everything went black around him as the city twisted like a kaleidoscope beneath his feet.

"Ow," said Barnaby Brocket.

"Hey, kid! You all right?"

Barnaby opened his eyes and looked up. He was hovering underneath a wire cage that was hanging off the side of the building, just where the upright walls gave way to the terraced crown. Through the gaps in the grilled floor, he could see a pair of sturdy black boots.

"Say something, kid! Are you hurt?"

"Urgh," groaned Barnaby, looking up into the cage itself, where a young man in a pair of blue denim overalls was standing surrounded by buckets and cloths. "What happened to me?"

"You came sailing up here like a balloon with the air let out," replied the young man. "Then crashed into me and hit your head. How'd you do that anyway?"

"I float," said Barnaby, making eye contact with a passing hawk that was winging its way down toward

Elevating to the top of the CHRYSLER

the Hudson; he couldn't help but envy its ability to soar and land at will.

"No kidding!"

Barnaby tried to shrug, but his shoulders were pressed against the latticed floor, which made moving a little difficult. "Will you help me inside your cage?" he asked.

"Of course," said the young man, reaching over the side and taking hold of Barnaby's ears to pull him in and then keeping his hands pressed firmly on the boy's shoulders to stop him from floating away again. "This is a first," he said, shaking his head in disbelief. "I don't normally get visitors up here."

"You're a window cleaner?" asked Barnaby, looking around at the various scrubbers, squeegees, scrapers, and sponges that littered the floor of the cage.

"That's the day job anyway. Stops me from going hungry."

Barnaby craned his neck and stared up toward the top of the building, tilting his head to get a better view of the triangular windows and the ribbed steel arches that surrounded them.

"Impressive, isn't it? It takes me a whole week to clean them all, you know. The name's Joshua, by the way," the young man added, extending his hand. "Joshua Pruitt."

"Barnaby Brocket," said Barnaby.

"That's some nasty bump you've got on your

head," said Joshua, parting Barnaby's hair a little with his fingers. "We need to clean that up a little. You want to come back down with me?"

Barnaby looked around. He didn't have much choice, really; it was either go back down to street level or float away into the sky. "All right, then," he said.

Joshua nodded and lifted a metal brick that was hanging from the side of the cage walls, slapped his hand down on a large green button, and they began to descend. He kept a tight hold of Barnaby's hand as they went round the corner and entered the building through the service entrance, crossing the floor toward a single gray lift. Once inside, he pressed the button marked –3 and they began to descend into the depths of the building.

Leaving the lift, they made their way along a twisty corridor with gray stone walls covered in ancient-looking pipes that made strange gurgling sounds as they passed by before descending a short flight of uneven steps and opening a large metal door that led into a dark and gloomy room. Joshua pulled a cord, and a single lightbulb illuminated what appeared to be someone's makeshift home. In the corner was a sleeping bag, and next to it some empty cups, a couple of books, and a half-eaten sandwich.

"Sorry about the mess," said Joshua, looking a

little embarrassed. "I don't tidy up as much as I should."

"Do you live down here?" asked Barnaby.

"Sure do. I can't afford my own place, so I thought I'd stay here for a while." He scratched his head and looked a little unhappy that this was the best that life was offering him. "It's better than paying rent for some tiny box on the opposite side of the city."

Barnaby wondered what might lead to someone living underneath a building like this—and where the young man's parents were. *Will I end up in a place like this?* he asked himself as Joshua rummaged in a box in the corner of the room and pulled out a bottle of something green and gloopy-looking and a couple of Band-Aids. *What if I never make it home at all?*

"Good as new," said Joshua, dabbing the disinfectant on Barnaby's head with a cotton ball and crossing the Band-Aids in an X shape over the bruise. "You feel better now?"

"Much better," said Barnaby. He sat down on one of the large round pipes that ran along the base of the walls and held on to it tightly, as the ceiling was made almost entirely of steel. It was at moments like this that he longed for his David Jones Bellissimo plush medium mattress.

"Okay, Barnaby," said Joshua. "Let me just put these things away and we'll get you back upstairs."

As he disappeared round a corner, Barnaby's attention was taken by an open door on the opposite side of the room. He stood up and made his way carefully toward it, holding on to the steel girders like a monkey swinging from vine to vine. Scattered around the floor of the next room was a most unusual collection of sculptures, all made out of iron and twisted into strange but interesting shapes, some with strips of wood buried in the center, their wooden hearts flecked with an icy blue paint. There didn't seem to be any particular sense to the designs, and each one was different from the next, but when he picked one up, he was intrigued by the object he was holding; they looked like pieces you might find in an art gallery or a museum.

A moment later, his attention was taken by something equally unexpected that sat in the corner of the room: a simple cardboard box filled to the brim with cotton swabs—the type you soften in water to clean your ears. There must have been thousands of them in there. Tens of thousands.

"I thought you'd floated away," said a voice from behind him, and he spun round to see Joshua, who'd followed him inside.

"Did you do these?" asked Barnaby, looking around at the sculptures.

"Sure did. You like them?"

"They're really good. What do they mean?"

"You have to decide that for yourself. Each one means something different to me. I told you that being a window cleaner was only my day job. I'm an artist, really. Or I want to be anyway. Not that I can get anyone to look at my work or buy it. You have no idea how snooty all the gallery owners in this city are. Maybe I'm wasting my time, I don't know."

"And what about the box of cotton swabs?" asked Barnaby. "Are they art too?"

"No," said Joshua, smiling. "No, that's just a box of cotton swabs."

"You must have very dirty ears."

"They're not for me," he replied, picking one up and staring at it. "I just keep them to remember my family by. It can get pretty lonely this far underground, you know."

"Most people keep photographs," said Barnaby.

"Well, I've got one or two of those in my wallet too. But the family business is cotton swabs, so they remind me of home. My father's the cotton-swab king of America. Which makes me the prince, I guess. You ever heard of Samuel Pruitt?"

Barnaby shook his head.

"Well, I suppose he isn't very famous. But he's very, very rich. He invented the cotton swab. And anytime anyone in the world buys a pack of swabs to clean out their ears, my father makes a quarter. That's a lot of quarters. Put them all together and they make a lot of dollars."

"So why do you live down here?" asked Barnaby. "You must be able to afford to live in a palace."

"That's my father's money," said Joshua, steering Barnaby back toward the corridor. "It's not mine. The only money I have is whatever I make out of washing those windows. It's enough, though. It keeps me from starving while I'm working on my art. He cut me off without a dime. Won't let me in the house. Won't have anything to do with me."

"But why not?" asked Barnaby as they went back up in the lift. "Hasn't he seen how good your sculptures are?"

"He's not really an art lover, that's the problem. He's only interested in money. And that's what he wanted me to be interested in too. He tried to teach me the cotton-swab business; he wanted me to come to work for him, and then when he retired, I was meant to take over. But you want to know a secret? Cotton swabs—they're not that interesting."

"I suppose not."

"And, anyway, I wanted to do what *I* wanted to do with my life. Not what someone else wanted me to do with it. So here I am, living like a rat, spending every night working on these pieces and starting to think that maybe he was right all along. No one's ever going to take me seriously. Maybe I should pack it all in."

They were back on the street now, and Joshua

handed across a pair of iron weights that he'd taken from the underground room.

"Slip these into your shoes," he said, not noticing that Barnaby had also taken something and hidden it in his back pocket. "It'll be difficult to walk with them, but at least they should stop you from floating away for a little while."

"Thanks," said Barnaby. "And thanks for fixing my head too. Most people wouldn't have cared."

"Most people are a lot of hard work," said Joshua, waving a hand in the air as he climbed into his window-washing unit, pressed the green button, and started to rise once again. "Take care of yourself, Barnaby Brocket. New York can be a pretty dangerous place, you know!"

Chapter 12

A Star Is Born

Barnaby stopped thinking about how to get home to Sydney and started thinking about how to thank Joshua Pruitt. Very few people, he decided, would have been thoughtful enough to disinfect his bruise and make sure that he wouldn't float away. But what could he do? he wondered. He had very little money and no friends in the city.

And then he had an idea.

Walking slowly down the street—*very* slowly—he went in search of a post office, and when he found one, he stepped inside and sat down on a stool in front of a large telephone directory, turning the pages quickly as he searched for the address. It didn't take him long to find what he was looking for. He scribbled the details down on a piece of paper and, because most of the streets in Manhattan are numbered instead of named, he made his way there with very little difficulty, despite the iron weights in his shoes and the fact that his ears were starting to hurt again.

From the street outside, the art gallery looked very imposing. It was painted completely white, and through the large windows Barnaby could see only a few small paintings hanging on the walls. He had never been inside such a place before and felt a little anxious, but he took a deep breath, opened the door, and stepped inside.

A woman seated behind a desk looked up; when she caught sight of him, the expression on her face suggested to Barnaby that she might be about to pass out in horror.

"Revolting," she said in a surprisingly masculine voice.

"What is?" asked Barnaby.

"Your clothes. No feeling for color, no awareness of what's in and what's out. I mean—checked shorts at this time of year," she added, looking at Barnaby's outfit and shaking her head in disdain. "Where are we anyway, a golf course?"

She stood up, and he was amazed to see how tall she was—almost seven feet in height—with hair pulled back from her forehead so tightly that her eyebrows were raised up almost as high as her hairline. Her skin was deathly pale and her lips painted the most terrifying shade of blood-red.

"And who might you be?" she asked, dragging

out each word as if their enunciation was painful to her.

"I'm Barnaby Brocket," said Barnaby.

"Well, this is not a crèche, Benjamin Blewitt," she declared, her tone suggesting that it would be beneath her dignity to get the boy's name right. "Nor is it an orphanage. This is an art gallery. Get out immediately and take your peculiar smell with you."

Barnaby gave himself a little sniff, just like Captain W. E. Johns always did when he curled up in a ball in his basket, and realized that she might have a point there. He hadn't had a wash since leaving Ethel and Marjorie's coffee farm, and had slept on a train from Brazil to New York in the meantime.

"That's not a peculiar smell," said Barnaby, trying his hardest to sound offended. "It's my aftershave."

"You're too young to shave. You're just a little boy."

Barnaby frowned. She was right. It was best to simply get to the matter at hand. "I've come to see Mr. Vincente," he said.

"Mr. Vincente?" asked the woman, laughing at the absurdity of his remark. "Firstly, no one refers to him as *Mr.* Vincente; he is simply 'Vincente.' And secondly, I'm afraid that Vincente is extremely busy. His calendar is tied up from now until the end of the decade. And regardless of this, he does not associate with smelly little boys who wander in off the streets with Band-Aids on their foreheads."

"Please tell him that Barnaby Brocket is here," said Barnaby, ignoring her rudeness. "I'm sure he will want to see me."

"No. Now get out."

"Tell him that it is a matter of some urgency."

"If you don't leave," declared the woman, stepping forward now and towering over him, "I will be forced to call the police."

"Tell him that I have arrived from a certain coffee farm in Brazil. I think he'll want to see me then, don't you?"

The woman hesitated; she knew enough of her employer's history to realize that the words *coffee farm* and *Brazil* played an important part in it. She had read the biographies that had been written about him, after all, and every newspaper interview he had ever given. Perhaps this boy was *somebody,* she thought. Perhaps it might not be a good idea to antagonize him any further.

"Wait here a moment," she said, allowing an exhausted sigh to escape her mouth as she turned round and disappeared into an office at the back of the gallery.

A minute or two later, a dark-haired man with a pencil-thin mustache appeared, looking at Barnaby with a half smile on his face and an expression of some curiosity. "You wanted to see me?" he asked, his accent betraying his roots in the favelas of São Paulo.

"I'm Barnaby Brocket," explained Barnaby. "I was floating in the skies over Sydney when I bumped into a hot-air balloon piloted by your friends Ethel and Marjorie. It's a long story, but they took me to stay with them on their coffee farm for a week. I even slept in your old room. They speak very highly of you. Palmira told me that you were their favorite person ever."

"But they were my greatest friends!" exclaimed Vincente, clapping his hands together in delight. "My benefactors. Everything I have I owe to them. And they saved you too, yes? Like they saved me?"

"Well, sort of, I suppose," admitted Barnaby. "I certainly don't know what would have become of me if I hadn't run into them when I did." He looked over at the tall woman, who was glaring at him with a mixture of hostility and contempt. "Is this your wife?" he asked Vincente in an innocent voice. At this question her eyes opened so wide that Barnaby was afraid they might fall out and bounce across the floor.

"I am no man's wife," she insisted haughtily, as if she had just been accused of spending her evenings playing computer games.

"No," muttered Barnaby, shaking his head. "No, I thought not."

"But what can I do for you?" asked Vincente, taking the boy by the arm and leading him toward a beautifully upholstered sofa. "Ethel and Marjorie—they're not ill, are they?"

"No," said Barnaby, shaking his head quickly. "No, they're very well indeed. The thing is, Mr. Vincente—"

"Just Vincente, please."

"The thing is, Vincente, I'm right in thinking that you know all about art, aren't I?"

The gallery owner extended his hands and looked around at the items that were on display. "I know a little," he said modestly.

"Could I show you something and then you can tell me if it's any good or not?"

"No appraisals today!" insisted Vincente's assistant, clapping her hands sharply. "You need to make an appointment. I believe we have an opening on the second Tuesday of April, eighteen years from now. Shall I put you in for ten a.m.?"

"Please, Alabaster," said Vincente, silencing her with a stern expression. "If this boy is a friend of Ethel and Marjorie's, then he is a friend of mine. Come, Barnaby. What is it you'd like to show me?"

Barnaby reached into his rucksack and removed one of Joshua's sculptures—a small one that he'd taken without permission with this very plan in mind. He knew he wasn't supposed to take things that didn't belong to him, but he thought that, on this occasion, it might be all right.

Vincente took the piece of metalwork from Barnaby, turned it over in his hands, and stared at it for a minute or two before walking toward the window and examining it closer in the bright sunlight that was pouring through. He muttered something under his breath, then ran his fingers along the iron and wood before shaking his head in wonder.

"Exquisite," he said, returning to the boy. "Simply exquisite. Did you create this?"

"No," said Barnaby. "A friend of mine did. He's a window cleaner on the Chrysler Building, but he wants to be an artist. Only no one will look at his work. He disinfected my bruise and put Band-Aids on my forehead. I thought I owed him a favor in return."

"He does not *want* to be an artist," roared Vincente in a dramatic tone. "He *is* an artist! An extraordinary artist. But you must take me to him, you foul-smelling little fellow. Take me to him now!"

A week later, having taken advantage of Vincente's generosity in the shape of one of the guest rooms in his enormous apartment on Fifth Avenue, which looked down over Central Park, Barnaby—clean now, fully washed, scrubbed, and deodorized—arrived at the gallery wearing a pair of very expensive shoes with weights in the heels to keep him grounded, and made his way through the lines of photographers and newspaper reporters attending Joshua Pruitt's first show, an event that was being heralded by the art world as one of the most important of the year.

"I hear you're responsible for all this," said a man with a press badge, approaching Barnaby, who nodded and tried not to stare too much at the terrible burn marks that covered most of the man's face. He knew it would be rude to gawp at them but couldn't help wondering how they had come to be there.

"Sort of," said Barnaby.

"The name's Charles Etheridge," said the man, shaking Barnaby's hand. "Chief art critic with the *Toronto Star.* I heard all about this remarkable new work from Vincente and had to come see for myself. And it wasn't a wasted trip. I've got to take the train back to Canada tomorrow morning, but I'm glad I came. Speaking on behalf of my readers, I want to thank you for bringing young Mr. Pruitt's work to the attention of the world. We owe you a debt of gratitude. If there's ever anything I can do for you, just let me know, all right?"

Barnaby nodded, unable to think of anything that Mr. Etheridge really could do for him, and wandered off to find the artist.

"I can't thank you enough, kid," said Joshua, delighted by all the praise he was receiving. "And look over there—even my old man showed up. Seems like he's proud of me now that I've made it into the *New York Times* and says it's okay for me not to work in the cotton-swab business after all."

"So you're friends again?" asked Barnaby.

"Well, we've still got a lot of things to sort out. After all, he kicked me out onto the streets without a penny to my name. And why? Just 'cause I was a little different than he wanted me to be. I'll get over it in time, I guess, but it's not easy to forget. What kind of parent just tosses their son out of the house like that?"

Barnaby frowned and bit his lip. In all the excitement of the last week, he had not given as much thought to Alistair and Eleanor as he should have, but hearing Joshua say this made him think of home, although not in a good way. He glanced around at the extraordinary display that Vincente had set up, and at the wealthy art lovers examining each of the pieces as Alabaster stuck little red circles beside them to indicate that they were sold.

"We'll figure it out," continued Joshua. "As long as he realizes that I'm an artist, not a businessman. But what about you, Barnaby? What are you gonna do now?"

"I'm trying to get home to Sydney," said Barnaby. "I just have to figure out how."

And then an idea struck him. He walked back over to Charles Etheridge, the journalist from the *Toronto Star,* the one who had said that the world owed Barnaby a favor.

"Excuse me, Mr. Etheridge," he said. "You said you're going back to Toronto tomorrow morning?"

"That's right, young man. Why do you ask?"

Barnaby thought about it and tried to picture a map of the world in his head. "Is Toronto anywhere near Sydney?" he asked.

POST CARD

THE ADDRESS TO BE WRITTEN ON THIS SIDE

5-PM

Dear Family,

The plan was to fly from Brazil to Sydney but I fell asleep on a train and woke up in NEW YORK, which is why I'm not home yet, just in case you were worrying about me. I made some new friends in America but I'm on my way to CANADA today to fly home from there. A Newspaper is going to buy me an air ticket because they owe me a BIG thank you but they say I have to fly out of Toronto.

I'm still not having any luck trying to not float. ~~may~~ maybe thats just who I am. Tell Captain W.E Johns not to eat too many dog biscuits; he was getting a bit PORKY when I left.

Your son / brother / master

Barnaby

Mr & Mrs Brocket,
Henry, Melanie and
Captain W.E. Johns
15 Waruda Street
KIRRIBILLI
NSW 2061
Australia

Chapter 13

Little Miss Kirribilli

Eleanor was coming back from her walk with Captain W. E. Johns when she ran into the postman on the street. He handed her a parcel from a bookshop, a letter from Henry's school, and Barnaby's latest postcard. She read the letter first—apparently, Henry had been getting into fights over the last few weeks—and then hesitantly began to read the postcard. She could feel the blood draining from her face as she recognized her younger son's tone and felt an ache inside her unlike any she had ever felt before.

It had been weeks now since she had walked across the Harbour Bridge with Barnaby, and the events of that day were rarely far from her mind. There were moments when she thought she had done the right thing, because, after all, he was the most willful little boy who absolutely refused to change, but then, just occasionally, she wondered why it was that she had been unable to love him exactly the way he was. After all, she had always taken pride in the fact that she was a normal mother with an entirely normal family, but was it normal to do what she had done?

Across the street she saw Esther Frederickson getting out of her car with her seven-year-old daughter Tania in tow.

"Oh, hello, Eleanor," cried Mrs. Frederickson, turning round and waving an enormous trophy in the air. "First place!" she declared triumphantly. "Little Miss Kirribilli, just like her three elder sisters before her. And her mother!"

Eleanor smiled but couldn't bring herself to go over to congratulate Tania or Esther. The Little Miss Kirribilli contest brought up nothing but bad memories for her. When Eleanor was a girl, she had won the title of Little Miss Beacon Hill, and she'd hated all the fuss and attention that had gone with the crown. Her mother had been Little Miss Beacon Hill too, and from the day Eleanor was born, she'd used her daughter as if she was a dummy in a training school for makeup artists and hair stylists, covering her face with lipstick and rouge, piling her hair up in ever more extravagant bundles on her head, forcing her to walk up and down with her hands on her hips until she had perfected what Mrs. Bullingham, Eleanor's mother, described as her "signature walk."

"Now remember," she instructed her daughter

when she was only five years old and entering her first beauty pageant. "If the judges ask you what you want most in all the world, what do you say?"

"That I want to work in a kennel," said Eleanor. "And I want to rescue as many unwanted dogs as possible and find them good homes to live in."

"World peace!" cried Mrs. Bullingham, throwing her arms in the air. "Heavens above, child, how many times have I told you? The thing you want most in the world is world peace!"

"Oh," said Eleanor. "Of course. Sorry. I'll try to remember."

"And if they ask you who your best friend is, what do you say?"

Eleanor thought about it; this was an answer that changed quite regularly. "I think I'll say Aggie Trenton," she replied. "Last week it would have been Holly Montgomery, but she pulled my hair and stole my lunch on Tuesday."

"Your best friend is your mother," insisted Mrs. Bullingham through gritted teeth. "Repeat after me, Eleanor: *My best friend is my mother.*"

"My best friend is my mother," said Eleanor dutifully.

"Your favorite music?"

"The Beatles," said Eleanor.

"Chopin!"

"Oh yes. Chopin."

"Your favorite book?"

"Anne of Avonlea."

"Hmm," said Mrs. Bullingham, who never read any books at all. "All right, that answer sounds fine to me. Now, is there anything I've forgotten?"

Beauty pageants were never Eleanor's idea of fun. In fact, she hated having her makeup done and her hair styled; she much preferred going out into the neighborhood with the other boys and girls and getting messy and coming home with cuts on her elbows and mud on her face. But Mrs. Bullingham wouldn't allow that.

"You're a young lady," she told her daughter. "And you must behave like one. There are over forty different beauty pageants for girls your age in the state of New South Wales. If we put our minds to it, we can work the entire circuit and win every single one. Wouldn't that be wonderful? The most that's ever been won in a single season is thirty-six. And do you know who that was?"

"Who?"

"Me!"

Eleanor sighed. It wasn't just the pageants that she found boring, it was the other contestants too. Not one of the girls seemed to have a mind of her own. They repeated the things their mothers said and wore such wide smiles on their faces that it was a mystery how their cheeks didn't crack open.

But her mother offered her no choice. Weekend after weekend, they got in the car and traveled from Broken Hill in the west to Newcastle in the east, from Coffs Harbour in the north to Mornington Peninsula in the south, singing songs, marching up and down catwalks, winning trophies. Not once did Eleanor get to attend a friend's birthday party, because these always took place on a Saturday and that was the day she was in front of an audience, strutting her stuff.

This went on for six years until, just after her thirteenth birthday, Eleanor marched into the extension at the back of the house, which had been built especially to house her collection of trophies, and told her mother that her beauty pageant days were over.

"They're over when I say they're over," replied Mrs. Bullingham. "And that won't be until you've lost your looks. You've got another few years in you yet."

"I'm sorry, but no," said Eleanor calmly. "I won't go anymore. I hate those pageants. I don't like the way the people look at me."

"They're admiring you!"

"No they're not. It feels weird. I don't like the outfits, I don't like the competition, and I especially don't like the attention. Plus, they're bringing me out in spots, and the doctor says that's to do with all the anxiety I feel. The only thing I want is to be left alone."

And after a series of arguments, despite Mrs. Bullingham's threats, Eleanor finally got her way.

The makeup was thrown away, the inappropriate costumes were given to the Salvation Army, and Eleanor was left in peace at last.

If no one ever looks at me again for as long as I live, she wrote in her diary on the day that her trophies were all boxed up and put into storage, *then I think I will be able to grow old happy.*

She entered the house now, shaking her head to dismiss these thoughts, a part of her wanting to run across to little Tania Frederickson and tell her that she too could refuse to take part in the pageants if she wanted to. Nobody would think badly of her just because she wasn't this year's Little Miss Blue Mountains or Little Miss Woollongong.

But she didn't. Instead, she sat and read Barnaby's postcard again and allowed herself a long, deep sigh. Then, putting it aside, she opened the parcel from the bookshop—it was addressed to Barnaby—and took out a copy of *David Copperfield,* which he must have ordered before floating away. She stared at the cover for a moment—a young boy alone on a highway, a sign pointing to London, an expression of loneliness and anxiety on his face—before flipping to the opening pages.

Whether I shall turn out to be the hero of my own life, or whether that station will be held by anybody else, these pages must show.

"Bark," barked Captain W. E. Johns, who wanted to join her on the sofa, and she nodded, tapping the cushion beside her as she kicked off her shoes and stretched out.

To begin my life with the beginning of my life, she read, *I record that I was born (as I have been informed and believe) on a Friday, at twelve o'clock at night.*

Eleanor gave a little gasp when she read that line. Then she closed the book, stood up, and went into the kitchen, throwing Barnaby's postcard in the trash can. She opened the fridge and looked inside. *Pork chops for dinner,* she thought, pushing everything else to the back of her mind.

And pavlova for afters.

Chapter 14

The Photograph in the Newspaper

The following morning, Barnaby found himself back at Penn Station.

Standing on the terminal concourse, he glanced down at his feet, where a pattern of red and white lines panned across the floor, in sharp detail where he stood but fading a little to the left and right. He craned his neck and looked up at the windows behind him, where the morning sunlight was pouring through the base of the enormous Stars and Stripes flag, sending their colors floating down like a patriotic wave.

The station was filled with commuters, bleary-eyed and wet-haired in the morning rush hour, all carrying coffee in one hand and doughnut in the other; from their expressions you would have thought that if they failed to get where they were going immediately—or preferably sooner—then the entire universe would come to an end. They were *that* busy and *that* important.

Barnaby took a deep breath, then exhaled loudly as he watched the tourists milling around an information booth, arguing with the exhausted-looking woman cornered inside. On his back he was carrying a brand-new rucksack filled with old pieces of heavy iron from the basement of the Chrysler Building, which stopped him from rising off the ground and finding himself trapped under the concourse roof.

"Morning, Barnaby," said Charles Etheridge, marching toward him purposefully, carrying two bottles of water and a couple of apples; no coffee or cakes for him. Some of the people making their way into and out of the station stared at the terrible burn marks that covered his face, and looked away. Their cruel expressions might have hurt Charles's feelings had he not grown accustomed to being stared at. A teenage girl made a gagging sound, pointing a finger toward the center of her open mouth, and her friend burst out laughing; her screech made him look at her, and she flushed scarlet before turning away; she and her friend ran down the steps in fits of laughter.

"I brought you some breakfast," said Charles, his voice betraying a wounded awareness of what had just taken place. "I thought you might be hungry."

"Thanks," said Barnaby.

"And I collected our tickets on the way," he added, waving a couple of pieces of paper in the air. "We'd better hurry if we're going to make it in time."

They headed downstairs and zigzagged through a series of long corridors that led to the platforms. "You heard that young Mr. Pruitt sold all of his pieces last night, I suppose?" asked Charles. "And for a very tidy sum too. The *New Yorker* is running a major feature on the exhibition next week. And the *New York Times* is already preparing its list of reasons why it isn't as good as everyone says it is. He's the toast of the town and it's all down to you."

"I'm just glad he's going to be an artist after all," said Barnaby. "And that he's made up with his family."

"He was always an artist," replied Charles. "He's just going to be a very rich one, and in my experience the two don't necessarily go hand in hand."

They made their way to platform nine, where their train was waiting, and Barnaby looked across at the space that separated it from platform ten and narrowed his eyes.

"Wrong station," said Charles, noticing what the boy was doing.

"Just checking," said Barnaby, smiling as they boarded the train. Looking at the seats, he was pleased to see that he could stop himself from floating to the ceiling simply by buckling his seat belt around his waist, while Charles placed his rucksack on one of the overhead storage racks.

"That must get very awkward," said Charles. "The whole floating business, I mean. There must be so much you can't do."

"I suppose so," replied Barnaby as the whistle blew and the train began to pull out of the station. "Only I've never known anything different. Although there was this one time when I was climbing the Sydney Harbour Bridge with my class and we were all tied to the side in a long line, and for the first time in my life I was exactly the same as everyone else."

"And how did that feel?"

"Weird," said Barnaby, pulling a face. "I didn't feel like myself at all. I didn't enjoy it."

Charles nodded and stared at him for a moment, a half smile on his face, before laughing a little and opening his newspaper to scan the headlines. Barnaby looked out of the window and watched the scenery move past at high speed. He wished he'd brought a book with him. A little d'Artagnan would go down very well on a journey like this.

They were a few hours into their trip when the train pulled into Albany, where a group of passengers got off and a lot more got on. Barnaby watched as a handsome young man threw an enormous green haversack onto the overhead rack and sat in the seat in front. His nose was buried in a book, and Barnaby peered over to see the title: *A Nation of Politicians.*

"You don't have any adventure stories in that bag, I suppose?" asked Barnaby, leaning forward hopefully.

The young man turned round in surprise. "I don't, I'm afraid," he said. "I'm a history man. But I can give you something on land reform in early twentieth-century Ireland if you're interested. . . ."

Barnaby sighed and shook his head. He was in the mood for something with a chase in it. Or an orphan trying to make his own way in the world. Or a bit of fighting.

The carriage was quite busy by now, but there was a pair of free seats across the aisle, and a mother and daughter came toward them, hurrying to claim them. A relieved expression spread across the woman's face when she realized that she was not going to be standing in the aisle for the next three hundred miles. However, as they got closer, the little girl stopped in her tracks, took one look at the burns on Charles's face, and refused to move. Instead, her mouth dropped open, she stood stock-still, and looked as if she wasn't sure whether to scream or simply faint away.

"Move it, Betty-Ann," snapped the woman, noticing Charles too and shooting him an irritated glance, as if it was inconsiderate of him to sit in a railway carriage when he looked like that. "Betty-Ann, I said *move it*!"

Still, the little girl refused to take her seat.

HOW RUDE!

"Will you do as you're told, *please,*" insisted the woman, and this time she pushed her daughter forward, forcing her into the window seat while she took the aisle, with nothing more than the narrow corridor separating her from Charles.

Barnaby watched all this with great interest and then turned to look at his companion, who was busy reading an article, even though Barnaby was sure that he had seen him reading that very same page thoroughly about thirty minutes earlier.

Of course, when Barnaby had first met Charles the night before, he had been taken aback by the dark red scars and wrinkled skin that spread across his face from just below his right eye to the left-hand side of his chin. One of his ears looked rather grisly too, and there was a patch of clear white skin above his right eyebrow that appeared completely smooth. And even though he knew it was rude, he kept staring until Charles eventually put down the newspaper and turned to look at him.

"What?" he asked.

"Nothing," said Barnaby, flushing slightly and turning to stare out of the window again.

"You were looking at my face."

Barnaby glanced back and bit his lip. "I just . . . ," he began. "Well, I wondered what happened to you, that's all. Do you mind my asking?"

"No, I don't mind," said Charles, folding the

paper in half. "To be honest, I'd rather you asked me straight-out than just stared at me as if I was an animal in a zoo." He raised his voice a little for the benefit of Betty-Ann and her mother, who ignored him completely; by now the child was locked into a computer game and the mother was reading about celebrities. "And it's interesting that you ask now because I just noticed this."

He unfolded the paper and showed Barnaby a photograph in the "Style" section of a very beautiful young woman on a catwalk at a fashion show. Everyone in the audience was watching her with expressions such as mortals might have shown in ancient times when the gods descended to wander in their company; but the model simply stared down the lens of the camera with a look of bored disinterest on her face.

"Do you see this woman?" asked Charles, and Barnaby nodded. "You recognize her, I suppose?"

"No," said Barnaby, shaking his head.

"Really? You'd be about the only person in this carriage who doesn't. You've heard her name, surely? Eva Etheridge?"

Barnaby shrugged his shoulders, wondering whether he should just pretend. "Is she a model?" he asked.

"Is she a model?" asked Charles, laughing. "She's only one of the most famous models in the world. She's been the face of so many campaigns that even she's probably forgotten half of them. Not that she'd think of herself as *just* a model, of course. She's a singer too. An actress. A television personality. She has an underwear line designed specifically for other malnourished women. She's a spokesperson for any number of beauty products." He hesitated for a moment and shook his head, smiling a little. "Oh, and she's my sister," he added. "I almost forgot that."

Barnaby lifted the newspaper off Charles's lap and took another look, trying to see whether she bore any resemblance to the man seated beside him, but it was impossible to make out what he truly looked like beneath all those terrible scars.

"And these two people here . . . ," continued Charles, turning the page to a gallery of smaller photographs from the same fashion show. "These are my parents, Edward and Edwardine Etheridge. He's an extremely famous designer, and she's an equally successful photographer."

"But this show was on last night," said Barnaby, pointing at the date at the top of the page.

"That's right."

"And yet you went to Joshua's exhibition rather than that?"

"Of course I did."

"Didn't they invite you?"

"Oh, they invited me, all right," said Charles, his laugh a rather bitter one. "They always invite me to things now—ever since I became a famous art critic. But I never go."

"Why not?" asked Barnaby, frowning.

"There was a time when I needed them very badly and they weren't there for me," Charles replied, his tone filled with sorrow now. "They weren't interested in me at all until I was *somebody*. Now it just seems like too little, too late."

"But they're your family," said Barnaby.

"And look what *your* family did to you," said Charles, who had heard the story of the terrible thing that had happened at Mrs. Macquarie's Chair from both Vincente and Joshua Pruitt the night before. "You asked how I got my scars," he added, rubbing his eyes and sighing. "Are you sure you want to know?"

"If you don't mind telling me," said Barnaby, who *did* want to know.

"I don't mind telling you," said Charles. "But it's not a happy story and it doesn't have a happy ending."

"Most stories don't," said Barnaby. "I don't know how mine is going to turn out yet, but I'd like to hear yours."

Chapter 15

The Fire in the Studio

Darkness began to fall on the landscape outside, and some of the people in the carriage turned on the tiny spotlights above their heads in order to continue reading or turned them off in an attempt to get some sleep.

"I was only a boy when the terrible thing that happened to me took place," said Charles, speaking quietly now as he thought about the past. "Only eight years old."

"I'm eight years old now," said Barnaby.

"Well, then, perhaps you'll understand how I felt. My mother, who you saw in the newspaper, ran a photography studio from our home in Brooklyn. She had the top floor of the house; the middle floor was where my parents, Eva, and I lived; and the ground floor was where my father designed his collections. Both my parents were very busy people. It often felt like they were at the heart of everything that went on in the city. They only associated with the most beautiful people—people like them, models with perfect faces, movie stars, and cultural icons. Their version of normal, no one else's. Famous actors, musicians, novelists, artists—they all came through our home on a daily basis, and only occasionally did either of my parents even notice that Eva and I lived there too."

"Is your sister older than you?" asked Barnaby.

"No, a couple of years younger. She's almost thirty now. Hence the look of dread on her face in that photograph. Anyway, a few weeks before my ninth birthday, I found myself alone in the house. This almost never happened, as it was more the center of a very particular universe than a family home, and I thought I'd do a little exploring. So I went upstairs to my mother's studio and started looking through the contact sheets because I knew she had lots of photographs of models with their clothes off. And I was starting to get very interested in photographs of models with their clothes off."

Barnaby sniggered to himself, and as he did so, one of the attendants came through the carriage carrying a large basket of treats and crying "Pretzels! Pretzels!" very loudly in a singsong voice, waking half the passengers. When she reached Charles, she did a double take and moved quickly past him, even though Barnaby would have quite liked some pretzels. He was starting to realize just how rude some people could be when they were confronted with someone who looked a little different.

"Anyway, there's a lot of equipment in a photography studio," continued Charles, who gave the impression that he hadn't noticed the snub even though Barnaby was certain that he had. "An extraordinary number of liquids and potions, toners, developing fluids, stuff like that. I was doing things I shouldn't have been doing, of course, and disaster was bound to strike. I knocked over a lamp, which fell onto a pile of film stock, and before I knew what was happening, the whole room was ablaze."

Barnaby gave a gasp and put a hand over his mouth. He remembered how terrifying it had been when the classroom at the Graveling Academy for Unwanted Children had caught fire; he had thought he was going to die—and he would have too if it hadn't been for the bravery of Liam McGonagall and his pincer hooks. For weeks afterward he'd had nightmares about being trapped by fire and not being able to float above it.

"Everything that follows is a little hard to remember," said Charles after a few moments, looking down at his lap rather than directly at Barnaby as he thought about that afternoon twenty-five years before. "The whole house went up quite quickly, I was told. But somehow one of the firefighters managed to get me out. When I woke up,

I found myself in hospital, in the burn unit, and this awful gel was spread all over my face. My skin was burning intensely beneath the ointment, and I was covered with a thick layer of bandages. It was the most excruciating agony. Weeks later, when I could finally sit up and see myself in the mirror, I looked like a mummy from ancient Egypt. It was awful. For a boy my age, it felt like the end of the world."

Barnaby thought of the mummies he'd read about in history class and tried to imagine what it would be like to be wrapped up like that; he wasn't able to.

"I was in hospital for months. And when they took the bandages off, I looked even worse than I do now, as the scars were still spreading and hadn't fully settled down yet. Even the nurses couldn't bear to look at me, and they were used to dealing with burn victims. So there were operations, operations, endless operations. I turned nine years old on the ward, and as I was growing, the skin on my face started to stretch too and my face only became worse. And my parents, who had always set so much store by physical beauty . . . well, they simply couldn't believe what their son looked like now. I started to realize that while at first they had come to visit me every day, their visits had begun to grow less frequent, and soon I was only seeing them once a week; then they began to take it in turns to come. My mother would say that my father had a collection to deliver, or my father would say that my mother was spending the day taking photographs of a group of film stars eating lunch together and comparing hairstyles. Eva never came, except once, when she screamed so loudly that she had to be taken away before she upset the other patients. Then the visits dwindled to once a month. Then they were replaced by phone calls. Then I got the occasional letter. And finally I stopped hearing from them altogether."

"But that's terrible," said Barnaby.

"I wasn't one of them anymore, you see," continued Charles. "I was too different. The hospital relocated me to a children's residential home, and it was as if my family had decided that I didn't exist. And so the morning I turned sixteen, I got up early, packed a bag, and moved to Canada. I started a new life there with people who saw who I was on the inside rather than this burned creature on the outside. I made a life for myself, and when I started to gain recognition in the circles my family moved in, that's when they got back in touch. Last year they even started talking about me in interviews. But I don't speak to them. I won't take their calls, I don't reply to their letters, and I certainly won't let them 'friend' me or whatever it is people do on their computers these days, however much effort they make."

Barnaby glanced at the photograph of the model once again—and it was true, she was very beautiful, but she looked miserable, as if there was something missing in her life. And when he turned the page to see the picture of Mr. and Mrs. Etheridge, they were deep in conversation with the head of the United Nations, but there was an unhappy expression on their faces too.

"How did you survive in Canada?" asked Barnaby, who suddenly felt very far from home and completely alone. "If you didn't know anyone, I mean."

"Sometimes there are lucky moments in life," replied Charles, looking out of the window now and smiling at a happy memory, stronger than those sad ones. "I saw an advertisement for a room to rent in the city, and for the next five or six years ended up living in the home of a wonderful Spanish couple who ran a veterinary practice from an office attached to their house. They had no children of their own and treated me like a son. They didn't care what I looked like, didn't mind that I was different. Why, if someone stared at me in the street, they would fly into a rage to defend me. They were good people. But look—we should get some sleep. It's getting late and we have a few hours to go yet. Are you tired?"

"I am, in fact," said Barnaby.

"Well, close your eyes, and when you wake up,

you'll be in Toronto, the most magnificent city in the world."

"Actually, that's Sydney," said Barnaby, feeling sleep begin to arrive already. "But it's a common mistake."

The train pulled into the station early the following morning, and Charles and Barnaby woke up, looking around with sleepy eyes as the conductor called out: "Toronto! Last stop!"

"Better put this on," said Charles, reaching up to the overhead rack for Barnaby's iron-weighted rucksack and helping him into it. They ignored Betty-Ann and her mother as they stepped off the train and made their way through the station and out onto the busy street, pleased to be able to stretch their legs again.

"We'll hail you a taxi. All you have to do is ask for the International Airport," said Charles. "Here's your ticket. It's a long flight, I'm afraid, but at least you'll be on your way home."

"I don't mind," said Barnaby. "As long as I get there."

"I'm curious . . . ," said Charles, taking the boy aside and sitting down next to him on a bench. "I know what your parents did to you, and yet you still want to go home."

"Of course I do," said Barnaby.

"But why—when they sent you away like they did?"

"Because they're my family," said Barnaby with a shrug.

"But they didn't want you."

"But they're still my family," repeated Barnaby, as if this was the most obvious thing in the world. "And it's not like I'm ever going to have another mum and dad, is it?"

Charles nodded and thought about this. "And what if they send you away again?" he asked, and Barnaby frowned.

"I don't know," he said. "I haven't thought that far ahead. All I *do* know is that they're in Sydney, and no matter what they did to me, I still want to go home. Maybe they'll tell me they're sorry. And maybe they'll even mean it. If they do that much, well, then, that will probably be enough for me. Everyone makes mistakes, don't they?"

Charles smiled but was unable to argue with the boy's simple logic. "All right, then," he said, standing up. "Let's get you that taxi."

He put his hand in the air and one pulled over almost immediately.

Barnaby jumped in. "Thanks again," he said.

"You're welcome. Have a safe flight home."

The taxi drove off and Barnaby looked round, expecting to see Charles making his way toward his office, but to his surprise, his friend had sat down again and was looking at his mobile phone. His fingers hovered over it for a long time before he seemed to make a decision and started dialing a number.

Barnaby smiled and turned round again, sure that Charles and his family would soon be reunited, just like he would be with his.

And it was at that moment that his heart skipped a little beat as he realized that he had his rucksack, he had his iron weights, he had his plane ticket . . . but there was one very important thing that he didn't have that he would most certainly need for this taxi driver.

"I don't have any money," he said aloud, and a moment later the taxi had pulled in to the curb, the back door was opened, and Barnaby Brocket was promptly pushed out again onto an unfamiliar Canadian street.

Chapter 16

The Little Jelly That Caused So Much Trouble

Before Barnaby could even think what to do next, a great crowd started to sweep along the street toward him. There were hundreds of people, all wearing identical blue-and-white shirts with a large *A* in the center. He fell among them, clutching his rucksack firmly on his back as they passed the harborfront on the left before taking a sharp right turn, whereupon the entire throng began to pour into an enormous sports stadium with an open roof. As the fans dispersed to different parts of the arena, Barnaby found an empty seat at the end of a row and looked up toward the magnificent tower that stood next to the stadium, its great spire pushing up into the sky above.

Barnaby had always loved sport, although he'd never once been taken to a football match—Eleanor said that normal people did not want to have their afternoon spoiled by a little boy floating out of his seat and obstructing their view. So he usually only got to watch it on television, trying to keep track of the action as he lay pressed against his mattress on the living-room ceiling.

As the stadium began to fill up, Barnaby pulled a postcard out of his rucksack and started to write. He was only halfway through when a family squeezed past him and took the next three seats—two enormous parents and a rather skinny little boy of around Barnaby's age. All three were carrying so much food—giant cartons of popcorn, a couple of dozen hot dogs, liters and liters of fizzy drinks, bags of chocolates and sweets—that Barnaby feared they might explode if they ate it all. He put the unfinished postcard in his back pocket, trying not to stare at them.

"Don't you have anything to eat?" asked the boy sitting next to him, and Barnaby shook his head.

"I don't have any money," he said.

"Well, you can have some of mine if you want," said the little boy, pushing some food Barnaby's way. "I'll never eat it all anyway. My parents always buy too much. They think there's something wrong with me because I'm so skinny. My name's Wilson Wendell."

"I'm Barnaby Brocket," said Barnaby, happy to take a carton of popcorn, some hot dogs, a bag of jellies, and a huge four-liter container of something black, cold, and sweet that he sucked through a straw and that sent a fizzy sensation through his body. In fact, the food was so heavy that Barnaby thought it might be safe to take his rucksack off, and he placed it under his feet.

"Eat your dinner, Wilson," said the boy's mother as she dug into the bottom of a bucket of popcorn for a finger-coating of salt.

"You're fading away," said the father, licking the ketchup-and-mustard mixture that had spilled onto the hot dog wrapper.

"I *am* eating," said Wilson, putting a single piece of popcorn in his mouth and chewing it carefully. "I hate all this junk," he added in a whisper, turning to Barnaby. "They won't be happy until I look just like them."

"Well, you can't eat like this all the time," agreed Barnaby, enjoying every bite. "But when you're hungry, like I am—"

"You have a funny accent," said Wilson, interrupting him. "What's the matter with your voice?"

"Nothing," said Barnaby. "I'm Australian."

"I have an aunt who lives in Melbourne," said Wilson. "Although I've never been there. Is it true that the water in the toilet goes the wrong way round there?"

"It depends what you think the right way is, I suppose," said Barnaby.

Wilson thought about this and gave a little grunt of agreement. "Who's your favorite football player?" he asked after a moment.

"Kieren Jack," said Barnaby, who had watched the number fifteen play many times on television and had a poster of him on his bedroom wall. "I'm a Sydney Swans man."

"Never heard of him," said Wilson. "Never heard of them either."

"Well, he's only the greatest footballer in the history of the world," said Barnaby.

"I like Cody Harper," said Wilson, pointing down at the team that had just run out onto the field—to massive cheers from the crowd. "The greatest kicker the Argonauts have ever had."

"Which one's he?" asked Barnaby.

"Number seven," said Wilson. "Although he's having a rotten season. The fans all want the manager to drop him. Not me, though. I know he'll come good one of these days. What the—?"

A great groan came from the crowd as the sky suddenly opened and the rain began. There was a powerful heaving sound, and the motors on either side of the open roof kicked into gear to close it. Barnaby looked up in disappointment. He quite liked being able to gaze up at the tower looming over them.

"That's where all the tourists go," said Wilson, seeing where Barnaby's eyes were focused. "They take the elevator to the top, then walk out onto a glass floor and look down over the city. One more jelly, I think," he added, reaching into the bag of sweets that was sitting on Barnaby's lap and picking out the smallest, most delicious-looking jelly. It couldn't have weighed more than a gram, but it must have been the difference between balancing Barnaby and unbalancing Barnaby, because the moment Wilson took it, Barnaby felt that familiar floating feeling begin to overtake him, and his legs started to rise off the ground.

"Uh-oh," he said, reaching down for his rucksack—but either he'd pushed it too far back under the seat or he'd already risen too high, because he couldn't grab it, and before long he was airborne.

"Fantastic!" cried Wilson as the rest of the crowd, even those on the field, turned to look up at Barnaby. Ignoring the commotion, Cody Harper scored a quick goal—his first in ages—but as no one witnessed it, it didn't count. And Barnaby's unfinished postcard fell out of his pocket and landed in Wilson's lap.

Barnaby heard the roar of the crowd and waved down to them, but their cheers soon turned into gasps, for as he rose higher, so the two sides of the roof were closing in on each other.

There were only three things that could happen now.

The first was that it would close before he reached the top.

The second was that Barnaby would make it through before they met.

The third—which was the worst option of all—was that it would close just as he got there and Barnaby Brocket would be sliced in two.

And unfortunately for him, that's exactly what happened.

Don't worry—it didn't.

For just at the moment when the two halves were about to seal the stadium, Barnaby slipped through the small gap that remained—a gap only big enough for an eight-year-old boy—and found himself looking down on the SkyDome from outside, the white roof growing smaller beneath him as he rose.

"Help!" he shouted, waving his hands toward the tourists in the tower; they all waved back as if this was just another entertainment laid on for them by the mayor of Toronto.

A small viewing platform at the top came into sight, and Barnaby noticed a black-suited figure running up the stairs inside and pulling open the door; he was carrying what looked like a fishing rod and casting it out into the air. It blew around in the wind, and Barnaby realized that it wasn't a fishing rod at all; it was a whip.

"Grab ahold of it!" shouted the man, and Barnaby pushed himself as hard as he could to the right as he reached out for it, catching it by his fingertips and holding on tightly as the man dragged him over the top of the rail and immediately sat on him so he couldn't float away again.

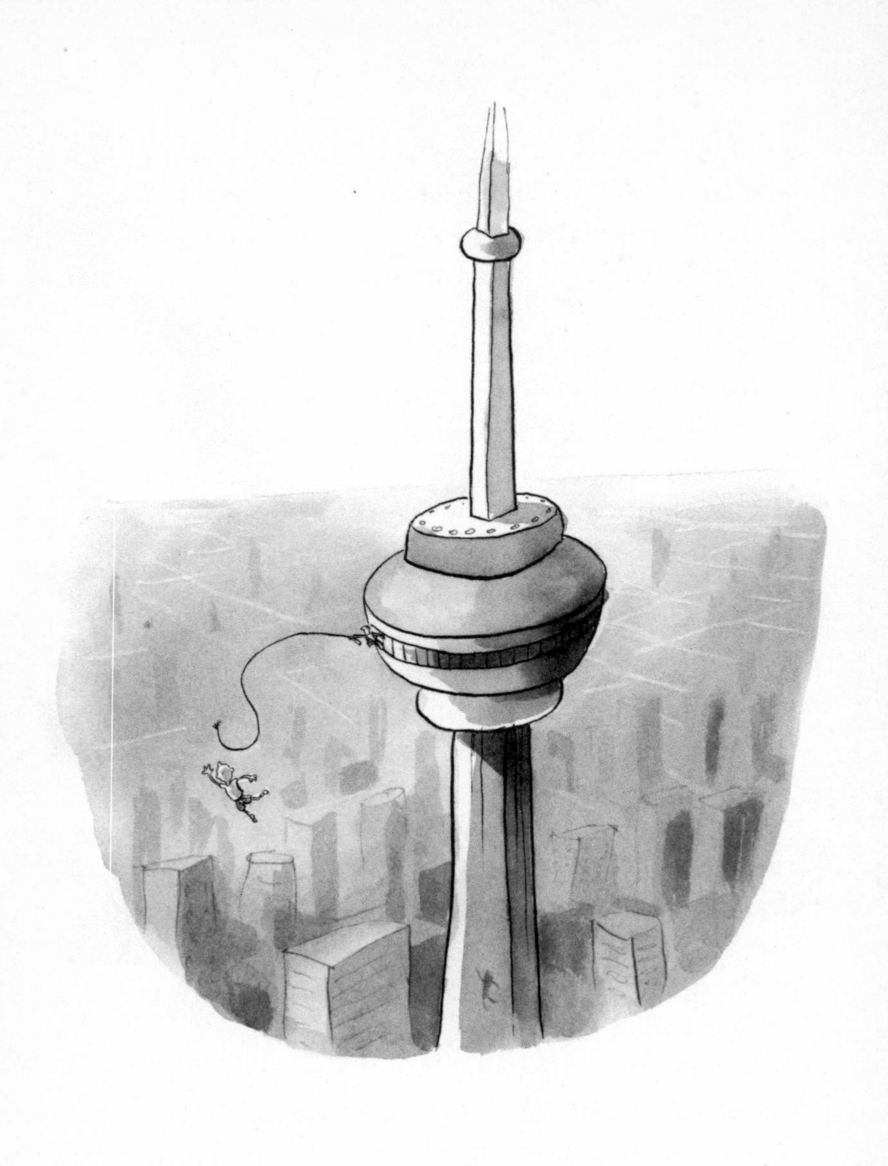

SAVED by the WHIP

"Thank you," said Barnaby, looking up in relief.

"You're very welcome," said the man, looking at the boy as if he wanted to eat him whole. "I saved your life, young man. That means it belongs to me now."

Barnaby stared at him in surprise.

"Just kidding," he said, smiling in a rather nasty way, and the tone of his voice made Barnaby think that he wasn't kidding at all. After a moment the man stood up, pulled the boy to his feet, and they went inside. Barnaby felt less than comfortable because the man had locked arms with him and was holding him very tightly so he couldn't escape even if he wanted to.

"What a trauma for you," he said, shaking his head. "Let's get you some water, shall we?"

"I'm fine," said Barnaby, thinking of all the planes in Toronto preparing to fly to the Southern Hemisphere. "I should be going, really."

"Nonsense," said the man. "Where would you go?"

"Home, of course," said Barnaby.

"And where is home?"

"Sydney, Australia."

The man smiled. "You're not from Toronto?" he asked.

"No. And could you let go of my arm, please? You're hurting me."

“Oh no, I couldn’t do that,” said the man. “You might float away on me again, and we can’t have that, can we? I told you, your life belongs to me now.”

“But you said you were kidding.”

“And I’m still kidding,” said the man with a nasty smile. He had a very pale face, greasy dark hair, and was dressed in what looked like a black tuxedo with red ribbing on the lapels. He made a funny cracking motion with his wrist, and the whip that he had used to reel Barnaby in rolled up perfectly as he returned it to a pouch beside his leg.

“Why do you carry a whip with you?” asked Barnaby.

“It’s part of my job. You’ve been to the circus, I presume?”

“No,” said Barnaby, shaking his head. Alistair wouldn’t let him go to the circus when it came to Sydney, for much the same reason that Eleanor wouldn’t let him go to football matches. “But I’ve seen one on television.”

“Well, I work in a circus. Of sorts,” explained the man. “A very special type of circus. I mean, we don’t have lions or tigers or clowns, nothing like that.”

“Then what type of circus is it?” asked Barnaby.

“Oh, that would be telling, wouldn’t it? Now here . . . ,” he said, opening a small bottle of water that he was carrying in his inside pocket and handing it across to Barnaby. "Drink this, why don't you? You'll feel better for it after all your excitement."

"But I'm not thirsty," said Barnaby. "And I haven't had any excitement."

"Drink it," repeated the man, and something in his tone made Barnaby feel that he'd better do as he was told or there might be trouble ahead. And so he lifted the bottle, put it to his lips, and swallowed it all in one draft. It tasted like regular water, only with a sort of sweet aroma and a bitter aftertaste. So actually, nothing like regular water, really. "Good boy," said the man, smiling again as he returned the empty bottle to his inside pocket. "Now, let's just wait a moment or two and then we can go."

Barnaby nodded and started to yawn; he was getting tired now. *I'll just wait until we stand up again,* he thought. *Then I'll thank the man for saving me and be on my way.*

But as he thought this, his eyelids became even heavier, his legs started to feel like jelly, and his head grew dizzy. He thought he was going to collapse onto the table, but before that could happen, the man picked him up and threw him over his shoulder.

The last thing he heard before he fell into a deep sleep was the man's voice calling, "Out of my way, please. My son has fallen ill," as he ran down the tower steps, circling over and over until all of Toronto seemed to disappear into a sort of dream world, a place that Barnaby could not have awoken from even if he'd wanted to.

POST CARD

CARTE POSTALE

THE PHOTOGELATINE ENGRAVING CO., LTD., TORONTO

Dear Family,

I've made it to
Toronto and later
to day I have a seat on a plane
flying to SYDNEY so hopefully
I won't be much longer getting home.
If my copy of David Copperfield
has arrived, can you put it on my
bed please. I don't want anyone
reading it and breaking the spine.
I'm at a ball game at the minute and
there's an open roof although it looks like
it might rain. I wanted to tell
you that

Mr & Mrs Brocket
Henry, Melanie and
Capt. W. E. Johns.
15 Waruda Street
Kirribilli
NSW 2061
AUSTRALIA

Chapter 17

The Postcard That Smelled Like Chicken

"Wanted to tell us what?" asked Henry, flipping the postcard over, looking for more.

"Well, I don't know what," said Melanie. "That's all it says. He must have stopped writing at that point."

Henry frowned. "But if he stopped writing, then why would he post it?" he asked. "Why wouldn't he finish it first? It doesn't make any sense."

"Well, *I* don't know," repeated Melanie. "Maybe something happened that meant he couldn't go on."

"Like what?"

"I don't know, Henry! It's a mystery. Anyway, we obviously weren't even supposed to find this postcard. It was crumpled up in the trash can."

"Is that why it smells of chicken?" he asked, giving it a little sniff before turning away in disdain.

"I assume so. I was throwing out some empty

cartons, and that's when I saw it. It must have arrived this morning, and either Mum or Dad threw it away."

"Which is very strange. I mean, it's a postcard from our only brother—"

"He's not *my* only brother," pointed out Melanie.

"Oh yes. Well, *my* only brother. And your second-favorite brother."

"Hmm," said Melanie, frowning a little as she considered this.

"So why wouldn't they want us to see it? They know how much we miss him."

Henry stood up and walked over to the bedroom window, staring down into the garden below. Captain W. E. Johns was out there, sniffing around the washing line where Barnaby had once been hung out to get some sun on his face. The dog had been very disconsolate these last few weeks. It didn't seem to matter what anyone did, it was obvious that he was missing his master. He wouldn't even let Alistair or Eleanor take him for walks anymore, staying in his basket until Henry or Melanie came home from school and then charging toward the front door, anxious for a run.

"The whole thing is distinctly odd," said Henry, turning back and glancing at his brother's empty bunk. "After all, if what they told us is true, then why wouldn't they want us to see his postcard? They know how worried we are about him."

"Of course what they told us is true," said Melanie, going over to examine her hair in the mirror. "It's not as if they sent Barnaby away themselves. He took his rucksack off, you know that. He was always complaining about it. Still, I suppose what matters is that he's trying to get home."

"It's a long way from Canada to Australia, though. We studied it in geography class. It's practically the other side of the world."

"Nowhere's difficult to get to these days," said Melanie. "Not with all the planes that go to and fro. Why, he could make it back to Sydney by tonight if he put his mind to it. He says he has a seat booked, after all."

"And yet I have a feeling that he won't."

"So do I."

The two siblings sat down on Barnaby's bunk, thinking through all the possibilities in their minds but unable to come up with a satisfying conclusion.

"I miss him," said Melanie eventually, sighing deeply.

"I do too," agreed Henry. "He wasn't a bad brother, all things considered."

"Personally, I always liked the fact that he floated. I never thought it made him different; I thought it made him special."

"Everyone I know admired him for it."

"Everyone except Mum and Dad."

"Yes, they hated it," agreed Henry. "Do you think if he comes back he'll still float?"

"I don't see why not."

"They won't be happy with that."

"But maybe they won't mind so much since they'll have him back safely. They must miss him as much as we do."

"If they do, they make a good job of hiding it."

"Oh, don't say that, Henry."

"Well, it's true, isn't it? After all, they don't seem very concerned, do they? If you ask me, they're happy that Barnaby is gone."

And with that, Henry leaned back on the bed, only to feel a curious bump under the duvet. He reached underneath and pulled out the bulky item that someone had left there for safekeeping.

David Copperfield.

"Oh," said Henry and Melanie, looking at each other in surprise and wondering what that could possibly mean.

Chapter 18

Freakitude

When Barnaby woke, he felt a great throbbing pain running from ear to ear. He lay quite still, hoping that he might fall straight back to sleep, but the floor beneath him was moving up and down in a rolling motion. As he stretched out, his hands and feet pressed against a set of bars and he realized to his horror that he was being held in some sort of cage.

"He's awake," said a voice to his left, and he looked round anxiously.

"Who's there?" he asked. "Where am I?"

"Don't worry, you're safe," said a second voice, and as Barnaby's eyes began to adjust to his gloomy surroundings, he saw that he was in a long, dark, windowless chamber, with just a couple of low-hanging lightbulbs to illuminate the space. Pressed against the walls was a row of empty cages similar to his own, and a small group of people were sitting on the floor, watching him.

"Don't be frightened," said a middle-aged man.

"You were captured," added a little girl standing next to him.

"Who are you?" asked Barnaby, and as he looked closer, he noticed the most extraordinary thing: the man had no ears and no nose but a wonderful bushy mustache, red in the center and auburn toward the ends, like all the colors of autumn gathered together in one place.

"Francis Delaware," replied the man. "At your service. And who might you be?"

"I'm Barnaby Brocket," said Barnaby.

"Well, Barnaby Brocket, you've got yourself into quite a pickle, haven't you? From what my friends and I can gather, you seem to have some difficulty staying on the ground. Problems with gravity—am I right?"

"Yes," said Barnaby, shrugging his shoulders apologetically.

"Well, you floated past the wrong man," said a boy of about sixteen, waddling over. Barnaby stared at him in amazement, for he had a set of flippers where his feet should have been. He was like a cross between a boy and a penguin. "Please don't stare," he added in a sad voice.

"I'm sorry," said Barnaby. "It's just that I've never seen anything quite like it before. And how can you hear me, Mr. Delaware, if you have no ears?"

"Your guess is as good as mine," he replied. "I might as well ask you how you can float. You don't know, do you?"

"No, it's a mystery."

"Would you like to come out of your cage?" asked the boy with the flippers, whose name was Jeremy, and Barnaby nodded. The door was opened for him; he stepped outside and immediately floated up to the ceiling.

"That must be terribly frustrating," said a young girl. Attached to her shoulder was her identical twin, of the Siamese variety.

"Terribly frustrating," repeated the twin.

"I've grown used to it," said Barnaby. "But you don't have anything around here that can keep me on the ground, do you?"

Francis Delaware scurried off for a moment and returned with what looked like a ball and chain. "Will this do?" he asked. "We could tie it to your leg."

"Perfect," said Barnaby as the others reached up to pull him down and then attached the chain to his ankle so that he was standing among them. "This is all very confusing," he went on. "The last thing I remember, I was floating up to the top of a tower, then a man saved me and gave me some water to drink."

"That wasn't water," said the little girl, Delilah, who didn't at first seem to have any unusual characteristics. "That's how he captured each one of us. We've all drunk that so-called water."

"Us?" asked Barnaby. "Who are you all anyway?"

"We are known," declared Francis Delaware, standing tall and sounding highly insulted, "as Freakitude."

"Freakitude?" asked Barnaby.

"It's offensive," said the second Siamese twin furiously.

"It's not even a proper collective noun," added the first.

A chorus of voices chimed in, each one stating how much more offended they were by the term than the last, and they were silenced only by the commanding tone of a rather pretty woman in a floral dress.

"Anyway, us calls he what that's," she declared. "It over control no have we, but course of demeaning it's."

"I beg your pardon," said Barnaby, blinking two or three times, unsure whether he'd just gone quite mad, as he hadn't understood a single word of what she'd said.

"Yes, I'm afraid Felicia takes a little getting used to," said Jeremy, the boy with the flippers. "Everything she says comes out backward. You have to listen back to front, if you can manage it. Or read her back to front if she writes something down. We barely notice, to be honest, we're

An odd collection

of FRiends

so accustomed to her way of talking. Strangely enough, when she sings, the words come out in the normal order."

"So why doesn't she sing rather than talk?" asked Barnaby.

"Oh, because she's a terrible singer. She'd bring tears to your eyes. And not in a good way either. Think nails on a blackboard."

"Sentences short in speak to try I'll," said Felicia, shrugging her shoulders. "Way that you for easier be might it."

"All right, then," said Barnaby, trying not to laugh even though it *was* rather funny, and then almost falling over. "Why does the room keep rocking back and forth like that?" he asked.

"It's not a room," said Jeremy. "It's a cabin."

"We're on a ship," said Francis Delaware.

"A ship?" asked Barnaby in surprise.

"Ship a," confirmed Felicia.

"Well, what are we doing on a ship?"

"Trying to escape from it," said a familiar voice, and a boy of around Barnaby's age appeared from out of the shadows. A perfectly normal boy—nothing out of the ordinary, except for the fact that he had two sets of neat steel hooks instead of hands.

"Liam McGonagall!" cried Barnaby, amazed and delighted to see his old friend from the Graveling Academy for Unwanted Children. He rushed forward to embrace him, but the ball and chain was too heavy and he fell face-first instead, landing on his nose on Jeremy's flippers, which smelled of sardines.

"Pick him up, someone, please," said Jeremy in a quiet voice, blushing furiously in the half-light. "This is terribly humiliating for both of us."

Several hands and hooks reached down to pull Barnaby to his feet.

"Hello, Barnaby," said Liam.

"What are you doing here?" asked Barnaby. "And how did I end up on a ship anyway?"

"Liam, you might as well tell him everything," said Francis. "From the top—there's a good boy."

The boy cleared his throat a little before he began. "The man who you met in Toronto is only one of the most despicable human beings ever to walk the face of the planet."

"No argument," said Jeremy.

"Terrible he's, oh."

"His name is Captain Elias Hoseason," continued Jeremy, "and at one point in his life he was a ringmaster in a circus."

At that moment, Delilah gave an enormous sneeze, and as she did so, she completely disappeared.

"Oh dear," said a voice coming from where she had been standing. Her own voice, in fact. "It's happened again, hasn't it? Does anyone have the smelling salts?"

Francis stepped forward, took a rather ornate silver box out of his inside pocket, opened it, and tipped a small quantity of something gray and powdery into his hand. He held it out before him and it immediately vanished, accompanied by a sniffing sound; then there was another tremendous sneeze and Delilah reappeared before them.

"Anyway," said Liam, raising his voice a little now, "if you're quite finished over there . . . As I was saying, Captain Hoseason was a ringmaster, but he grew bored with the animals and was looking for a little more excitement. And that was when he met Francis Delaware here."

"I was the first one," admitted Francis.

"Now, as you can see, Barnaby, Francis has no nose or ears and yet has perfect smell and hearing. To us, it's simply a fascinating trait in his character, but to Captain Hoseason he's a freak."

"He thought people would pay to see me," said Francis. "And he was right, they did. It was just the two of us for a while—not much income from that, of course—but then he met Delilah."

"I was the second," said Delilah. "He saw what happened when I sneeze, and he captured me too."

"Does it happen every time?" asked Barnaby.

"Every time. That's why I keep the smelling salts to hand. Or one of my friends here does anyway. I only need to sneeze again to immediately reappear."

"How peculiar," said Barnaby.

"It's her reality," insisted Jeremy, sounding wounded. "Please don't call her names."

"I didn't mean to. I only—"

"Would you like to hold my smelling salts, Barnaby?"

"Very much," he said, taking them and placing them in his inside pocket.

"It's her reality," repeated Jeremy, his face growing red again. "I won't stand for name-calling."

"He didn't mean anything by it," said Liam. "Now where was I? Oh yes. Then Captain Hoseason ran into Jeremy at an aquarium near Bristol. And as you can see . . ."

Jeremy looked down at his flippers and shook his head sadly.

"We were due to have an operation to separate us," said one of the Siamese twins.

"Only he kidnapped us from the hospital."

"Show radio my to listener regular a was he," said Felicia. "Night one home me followed he and. Head my over bag a threw. Too up locked was I knew I thing next."

"And what about you?" asked Barnaby, looking at Liam. "How did he capture you?"

"Well, after the fire at the Graveling Academy, my family and I moved to India. Freakitude played three nights at Habitat World, and he caught up with me on the street outside. He said I looked thirsty, offered me a drink of water, and the next thing I knew . . ." He looked at his surroundings and shrugged his shoulders.

"The point is, one way or another, he thinks we're all freaks," said Francis. "And as he captured more and more of us, he decided to go back into the circus game, only not with animals but with people instead. He must have thanked his lucky stars when he saw you floating up like that. Freaks like you—his word, not mine—don't appear every day."

"But it's not right!" cried Barnaby. "I'm not a freak! I'm Barnaby Brocket!"

"A boy who refuses to obey the law of gravity," said Delilah. "To Captain Hoseason, that's freakitude."

Barnaby stared around in dismay. "Well, what happens to us?" he asked. "And why are we on a ship?"

"We've been crossing the Atlantic Ocean since you arrived," said Francis. "We're on our way to Europe. Europeans love a good freak."

"Europe!" cried Barnaby, trying to picture a map of the world in his head. "Well, where in Europe exactly are we going?"

"I imagine we'll start in Ireland," said one of the twins.

"It is the first country you reach when you get to the far side," said the other.

"And is Ireland anywhere near Sydney?" asked Barnaby.

"Well, not really," replied Jeremy. "Although it's closer than Toronto was."

"And if you live in Sydney," said Francis, "then what were you doing in Toronto all on your own?"

Barnaby hesitated. He wasn't sure if he wanted to tell them about the terrible thing that happened at Mrs. Macquarie's Chair—but then, he thought, they had all been so honest with him about their unfortunate lives, it seemed only fair to be equally candid in return. And so he told them the full story.

"But that's terrible," said Francis.

"Shocking," agreed Felicia.

"Why would you want to go back to such despicable people?" asked Jeremy.

"Because it's home," said Barnaby, as if it was the most obvious thing in the world.

"Well, I hate to be the bearer of bad news," said Liam, coming over and placing a hook around Barnaby's shoulder, "but you won't be going back to Kirribilli anytime soon. Once Captain Hoseason captures us, he never lets us go. We'll be locked in our cages before we're allowed to disembark and then dragged in front of the next audience."

"But there's so many of you," said Barnaby. "And only one of him. Why do you let him do this?"

"The whip!" said Delilah, her eyes opening wide in horror.

"It's terribly painful," said Francis.

"Well, I won't do it," insisted Barnaby. "I won't be a freak."

"We're all freaks," said Jeremy.

"There's no escape."

"It of best the make to have just you."

"On the plus side," said Francis, tapping a finger against his chin thoughtfully, "we do get to see a lot of the world."

"I've seen quite enough of the world as it is," insisted Barnaby. "I've been to Brazil for a week, took a train all the way to New York, then another to Toronto, and now I'm on an ocean liner heading toward Ireland and—"

Barnaby didn't get to finish this sentence because just as he said the word *Ireland,* the ship came to a juddering halt and the engines were switched off. The small group gathered in a circle, holding their collective breath in anticipation, and a moment later they heard the sound of a hatch being opened directly above them. Daylight streamed in, and they turned their eyes away against the shock of the sudden brightness. When Barnaby managed to look up again, the only thing he saw was the face of Captain Hoseason grinning down at him.

"I see Sleeping Beauty has awoken," came the voice from above. "Now, are you all going to get into your cages and lock the doors like good little freaks, or do I have to come down there and sort you out myself?"

Chapter 19

Setting Free the Freaks

At Dún Laoghaire Harbour in Dublin, two long barriers had been erected on either side of the road. To the left a crowd of about two hundred people, freakophiles all, were waiting to see the extraordinary creatures who had made their way across the ocean. Opposite them stood a much smaller crowd, a quarter the size, made up mostly of students who waved placards in the air.

LET THE FREAKS GO FREE! said one.

IRELAND SAYS NO TO THE CAPTIVITY OF FREAKS! said a second.

STOP CALLING THEM FREAKS, THEY'RE JUST PEOPLE LIKE YOU AND ME, ALBEIT WITH SLIGHTLY DIFFERENT PHYSICAL CHARACTERISTICS AND IN ONE CASE A MOST UNUSUAL MANNER OF SPEAKING, said a third, held by a boy who didn't appear to understand how to make the most of his protest.

Both groups fell silent when a door was flung open on deck and Captain Hoseason appeared, looking resplendent in his freshly pressed ringmaster's outfit, a funereal black hat on his head, his whip locked carefully into the pouch at his side.

As he set foot on dry land, he indicated that the Gardaí might allow the television reporter and cameraman through for a short interview.

"Captain Hoseason," said a smartly dressed woman, thrusting a microphone between them. "Miriam O'Callaghan, RTÉ News. There's a large crowd gathered here today in protest at what they see as the forced imprisonment of freaks. How do you respond to this accusation?"

"With a sarcastic reply, of course," said Captain Hoseason, smiling at her. "And a patronizing aside to remark on your extraordinary beauty. Although this is hardly a large crowd, dear lady. The large crowd will be the one that gathers to see our wonderful performances over the next week. That crowd will put this crowd to shame."

"A lot of people feel that this form of forced servitude is genuinely unacceptable," continued Miriam. "Do you have anything to say to your critics?"

"I make a point of never listening to my critics," said Captain Hoseason, spreading his arms wide once again in a magnanimous gesture. "I find that they give me indigestion."

"But all these students who've taken time off from their studies—"

"My dear Miss O'Callaghan, do you really think that's what they'd be doing if they weren't here today? Let's be honest—if it wasn't me, they'd be protesting about something else. The latest war, the price of alcohol, giving women the vote, something like that."

"Captain Hoseason, here in Ireland women already have the vote."

"Do they indeed? What a very progressive nation you are."

"So you have no message for all these people who want to see the freaks set free?"

"Actually, I have four words," replied Captain Hoseason with a smile. "Over my dead body. And I have a wonderful new specimen that I picked up in Toronto only last week. A very interesting little fellow. Disobeys the law of gravity."

"Little boys can be terribly disobedient at times," cried one mother from behind the railings, looking down at her own son, who stared back up at her with an angry expression on his face. "They can be a curse."

"They can indeed, madam," replied Captain Hoseason. "They can indeed. But fortunately this boy is kept in a cage so the public is perfectly safe. And for only one hundred of your devalued Irish euros, you can view him for four nights in your capital city, Dublin, and three more in the town of Skibbereen in the People's Republic of Cork. Check the press for details. Until then, ladies and gentlemen, I bid you all good day."

And with that he made his way toward the front of a lorry as the last of the freaks' cages were loaded into the back—but before he could climb aboard, an elderly man rushed forward to shake his hand, locking him in a fierce embrace, and it took three Gardaí to pull him away. A little shaken, Captain Hoseason brushed himself down and was driven off into the Dublin afternoon.

"It sounded like there were some people on our side back there," said Francis as the lorry made its way through the city.

"They can't save us," said Liam. "No one can."

"The man's a monster," said Delilah.

"Tyrant despicable a," added Felicia.

Thirty minutes later the lorry came to a halt and the back doors were thrown open. A team of men were waiting for them, each wearing bright red polo shirts and yellow chinos, and they carried the cages into a specially constructed Portakabin where they looked at each freak with interest—particularly Jeremy, the boy with flippers where his feet should have been.

"You must be a great swimmer yourself, are you?" asked one of them.

"Your remark is both insensitive and ignorant," replied Jeremy.

"And you must be the new arrival," said

another, looking at Barnaby, who was lying flat against the top of his cage. "Look at you, you're floating!"

Barnaby stared at him and thought about happier times, like the day Captain W. E. Johns kicked a football past Henry into the goal in their back garden.

"Ah, don't look so miserable," said the man. "We've put something very special in here, just for you."

Inside the Portakabin, Barnaby was astonished to see that a mattress had been nailed to the ceiling in the corner, just like Alistair had done when he was a baby. The very sight of it made him long for home.

"Is it a David Jones Bellissimo plush medium mattress?" he asked hopefully.

"No, it's from the Argos economy line," replied the man, releasing the boy from his cage. "But it should do the trick."

"What a curious place," said Francis when they were alone, gazing out at the mansion where the president of Ireland lived.

"Look over there," said Delilah, pointing at the big top, which had been constructed in the center of the park with a sign that proclaimed FREAKITUDE! It was surrounded by caricatures of various strange-looking individuals, none of whom bore any resemblance to the people currently being held captive. “That’s where they’ll parade us like . . . like . . .”

“Like freaks,” said Jeremy, sitting down in a corner and burying his face in his flippers.

Later that night, however, after dinner, something unexpected happened. Captain Hoseason had been invited to dine with the president, who was intending to give him a stern lecture in two languages on how much he disapproved of what he was doing, and the freaks were gathered in a corner of the room playing cards, with Barnaby watching the action from above and trying not to shout out when he saw that someone had a particularly good hand. It was in the middle of a game of poker that they heard a curious scraping sound coming from the keyhole.

“What’s that?” asked Jeremy in fright.

They made their way back to their respective cages as the scraping continued—until finally the lock gave way and the door was flung open to reveal an elderly man: the same man who had thrown himself at Captain Hoseason earlier in the day.

“Hell’s bells!” cried the man triumphantly. “I did it!”

“Who are you?” asked Liam McGonagall.

“Shush, keep your voices down,” he said, poking his head back out of the door and looking around nervously. “Is everyone here?”

"Everyone *who*?" asked Barnaby.

"Everyone from the show. Everyone they call 'freaks,'" he added, looking a little embarrassed as he said the word.

"We're not performing for you now if that's what you're hoping for," said the first Siamese twin.

"Pay your money tomorrow night like everyone else," said the second.

"I don't want to see the show," said the man. "I've come to set you free."

"To set us free?" asked Francis, standing up.

"To set us free?" asked Jeremy, flapping his flippers.

"Free us set to?" asked Felicia, putting her hands to her mouth in delight.

"I read all about you in the paper," said the man. "And *Hell's bells!* I said to myself. *That's just completely wrong. Nobody should be kept in captivity like this.* You should be able to go home to your families. But we need to keep our voices down. There might be more security people around. We can't let them hear us."

"There's half a dozen outside somewhere," said Jeremy. "They've been there since we arrived this afternoon."

"Well, they're not there anymore," replied the man, laughing heartily as he held up an empty bottle in front of them—the same bottle that Captain Hoseason had offered to Barnaby when he took him inside the Toronto tower. "I stole this from that awful man earlier! Then I gave some to each of the guards. They should be out for the rest of the night."

"You managed to get them all to drink from that little bottle?" asked Francis in surprise.

"No, I bought a big box of doughnuts and sprinkled some of the water on top," he explained.

"That's *not* water," said Barnaby.

"Well, whatever it is. The point is, they're out for the count, and if you want to escape from this place, now's your chance. You want to go home, don't you?"

"I do," said Barnaby quickly. "I'm trying to get back to Sydney."

"Let's save the chitter-chatter for later," said the man. "We need to get going."

He opened the door and looked left and right. "You'd better jump on my back," he said to Barnaby. "We can't have you floating away. The rest of you, follow on behind."

Barnaby did as he was told, and a few minutes later the entire troupe was making its way through Phoenix Park in the moonlight. Two stags appeared in their path; stared at them for a moment, confused by the flippers, hooks, and—as there was a lot of pollen in the air—the woman who kept appearing and disappearing every few seconds; but in the end simply bowed their antlers and took off in the opposite direction.

In the distance, parked along the road, was a small fleet of cars and motorbikes. "I bought all these earlier today," said the man, chuckling away to himself. "Hell's bells, I have so much money it wasn't any problem at all. The students are going to take each of you in a different direction, so you'd better say your goodbyes now. That way, it'll be harder to track you down. We'll be heading for bus terminals, train stations, airports, and harbors. If you travel together, you'll stand out from the crowd too much."

Which, Barnaby thought, was what had got them into this situation in the first place.

The freaks all said goodbye to each other, promising to write once they got where they were going. Some of them had been together a long time, and although they were looking forward to going home, they were very sorry to be leaving the others behind.

"It was good seeing you again," said Liam McGonagall, offering his hook to Barnaby, who shook it warmly.

"Where will you go?" he asked.

"Back to India. If I can make my way there."

"I hope we meet again someday."

"Well, we didn't expect to meet this time, so you never know. Safe home, Barnaby!"

They sped off in different directions until there were only two people left by the final motorbike.

making a break

"You haven't told me your name yet," said Barnaby to the man who had saved them.

"Stanley Grout," he said. "And you'd better hold tight or you'll go shooting off into the night sky. These bikes go pretty fast, you know."

Barnaby did as he was told and locked his arms around Stanley's waist. "Where are we going anyway?" he shouted in his ear as they pulled out.

"The airport," he roared back, and twenty minutes later they were abandoning the bike in the car park.

"I bought a couple of tickets earlier," he said.

"To Sydney?"

"No, sorry. I didn't realize that was where you'd want to go. I'm on my way to Africa, so you'll have to come too, I'm afraid. But we can get you back to Australia once we arrive there."

Which was good enough for Barnaby. They went up the escalator toward departures, Barnaby clinging onto Stanley's back again as he didn't have any other way of staying on the ground.

"I'm too old for this," said Stanley a few minutes later, setting the boy down. "How are we going to keep you from floating away?"

"Rucksacks are best," explained Barnaby. "Filled with heavy items. I put them on my back and they keep me grounded."

"Right," said Stanley, leading the way to the shops, where he bought one—along with eight liter bottles of water, which they packed into the rucksack before strapping it onto Barnaby's back. And a few minutes later, Barnaby and Stanley were making their way down the ramp, boarding passes in hand. They found their seats, where they quickly fell asleep. And when they woke up again, they were already in Africa.

Chapter 20

Stanley's Wish List

"Six months," said Stanley the following afternoon as they made their way toward the Zambezi River, where the old man had an appointment scheduled for twelve noon precisely. "Does that seem like a long time to you?"

"A very long time," said Barnaby, who was only eight years old, after all, so six months accounted for one-sixteenth of his life to date.

"It's a blink of an eye," replied Stanley. "But it's all I've got left."

Barnaby stared at him, uncertain if the old man meant what he thought he meant. "You're dying?" he asked hesitantly.

"That's right. Two months ago the doctors gave me eight months to live, so I must be down to six now. I'd been having these terrible headaches, you see, so I had them checked out and they said there was nothing they could do for me. My number's up. And I said, *Well, if that's the case, then hell's bells, I'm going to live the way I want to live before I die.*"

"Is that what brought you to Ireland?"

"In a manner of speaking. I spent my whole life working. Built up one of the biggest businesses in America. Never took a day off. Never did a thing I wanted. Focused all the time on being on top, being number one, getting richer than the next guy. So when I found that I was on my way out, I thought, *If I don't do something for myself now, then I never will.* I made a list and started to tick things off one by one. My family came from Ireland originally and I'd never been back, so that's where I was last week. When I saw that freak-show circus—I tell you, Barnaby, I just about dropped dead right there in anger at the way you people were being treated and swore that I'd save every last one of you. And I did too! But that's not all. Over the past couple of months, I've scuba-dived off the Great Barrier Reef, walked a tightrope across Niagara Falls, rappelled down one of the Petronas Towers in Kuala Lumpur, and run with the bulls in Spain. And now I'm on my way—*we're* on our way—to the Victoria Falls Bridge for the world's biggest bungee jump. After that I plan to do a parachute jump. What do you think of that? You think I'm crazy?"

"Of course not!"

Stanley smiled and shook his head. "I wish everyone had such an open mind," he said. "My family say that I've gone gaga. Completely loony tunes. Crazier than a coyote in a chicken coop. They even tried to get me locked up. Here I am with only a few months left and they want me to spend my last days in some god-awful nursing home getting bed baths every day. How's that for a way to go? I told them, *Hell's bells, just let me have my fun,* but they wouldn't have it. They say it's not normal to be doing things like this at my time of life. *What's normal?* I asked them. *This!* they said, pointing at their own sorry lives. So I'm on the run. If they catch up with me, I'm toast."

"But don't you miss them?" asked Barnaby. "They are your family, after all."

"Sure I miss them," said Stanley. "I miss them every minute of the day. But I've spent my whole life in a three-piece suit. I've done what was expected of me. I've crushed my competitors and outfoxed my rivals. And do you know something? I haven't enjoyed a single minute of it. But these last two months? Pure pleasure. Every day. Now look ahead, Barnaby, my boy. Here we are."

They were standing close to a deep gorge on the Zambian side of the river. The Victoria Falls Bridge stretched out before them, a magnificent construct of shimmering steel, in the center of which stood the platform from which bungee jumpers made their leaps. They headed toward the platform, where a group of volunteers were helping to tie the harnesses. They looked at the old man and the boy and scratched their beards.

"Don't tell me I'm too old!" snapped Stanley, fixing them with a gaze that was as steely as the bridge they were standing on.

"And don't tell me I'm too young!" added Barnaby, who wasn't going to allow himself to be left out of this adventure.

The bungee assistants shrugged their shoulders and strapped the cords around the old man's legs as Barnaby held on to the side of the bridge to stop himself from floating away.

"Here goes nothing," said Stanley as he leaped off the platform and fell three hundred and sixty-five feet into the ravine, coming so close to the rocks and river below that Barnaby almost shouted out in horror; a moment later he bounced back up, went down, came back up again, down again, up again, over and over, until he was simply bobbing in the air, at which point he was dragged back to where he'd started.

"Hell's bells!" cried Stanley in delight, taking the goggles off. His thin hair was spread out at extraordinary angles, giving him a rather demented appearance. "If my kids could see the fun I'm having, they'd understand. What about it, Barnaby? You want to have a go?"

"Absolutely!" said Barnaby, allowing the volunteers to tie the cord around him now. He made his way to the edge of the platform, looked down, took a deep breath, and jumped; however, he only descended a couple of dozen feet before he started rising again—until the bungee cord was extended vertically into the clouds, with Barnaby at the end of it looking down rather than sinking into the gorge below.

"We should have seen that coming," said the old man, turning to explain things to the astonished people on the platform. "Kid refuses to obey the law of gravity. Better reel him in again."

A few minutes later Barnaby was winched back down and Stanley gave him his own bag to carry, as it held enough of his traveling gear to keep him grounded. "Sorry about that, Barnaby," he said, "but I don't think the bungee is for you. Maybe we'll have more luck with the parachute."

A private plane was waiting on a nearby runway, and they took off into the skies while a couple of instructors strapped parachutes to their backs.

"This is the big one," said Stanley, rubbing his hands together in glee as they ascended into the clouds. "The second last thing on my list. Once I do this, and then I do that, I'm through. You ready, Barnaby?"

"Ready!" said Barnaby, and they jumped out within a few seconds of each other.

Stanley sailed through the air, heading toward the ground and pulling the cord of his parachute at exactly the right moment. Barnaby, however, fell for no more than ten seconds before floating right back up again, at which point the plane circled around him with the door open until he could tumble back inside.

"I don't think parachuting is for me either," he said to Stanley when they were safely on the ground.

"Hell's bells, son, at least you gave it a try," said the old man.

That night, tired after their day's adventures, Barnaby and Stanley made their way through a forest, looking for a clearing in the trees.

"When I was a boy," explained Stanley as they walked along, "I always wanted to go camping and sleep out under the stars. But my dad—he was a railroad man—had to work every day and night to put food on the table, so I never got the chance. And when I had children of my own, I planned on taking them camping, but somehow work always got in the way. Big mistake on my part. So this is it, Barnaby, the last thing on my list. A night out camping under the stars. It'd be nice if my dad was here to share it with me, or my son, but one's long gone and the other's trying to have me locked up. So it's just you and me. What do you say—you up for it?"

Barnaby grinned and nodded his head happily. He was wearing a third, unopened parachute that the pilot had given him, which was so heavy that it was not only keeping him firmly on the ground but even making it a little difficult to walk.

It didn't take long for them to find a comfortable place to spend the night, and they threw a couple of waterproof mats on the ground and lay down, staring up at the stars. These were the same stars, Barnaby thought, that Captain W. E. Johns would be looking at now if he was outside in the back garden on private business.

"You're really going to go back to your family tomorrow?" asked Barnaby as they drifted off to sleep.

"I have to," said the old man, sounding a little sad but resigned to the inevitable. "I've done everything I wanted to do. And when I go, I'd rather go with the people I love by my side than in some country I don't know, all on my own. They'll be glad to have me back, but they won't understand why I had to do these things. I'm happy, though, and how many people can say that at the end of their days?"

Barnaby thought about this as he fell asleep, and he was so tired that he didn't even feel it when a fox appeared from out of the woods and chewed so hard at the cords of his parachute that he was able to drag it away into the forest, where he could dig his way to the center on what would be an unsuccessful forage for food. And he didn't notice when he drifted off the ground, rising up beside the trees as he floated into the night sky, which was empty now except for the stars and the moon in the distance.

Barnaby floated like this for a long time, and when he finally opened his eyes again, he was astonished to see that he was no longer lying on the ground. In fact, he couldn't even see the clearing anymore, or the old man, or the trees that surrounded them. When he looked down, he could make out the rivers and mountain ranges they had passed by earlier, and then he floated some more and realized that the shape he was looking down on was the outline of the African continent itself, so much bigger than he realized in comparison to the other continents—bigger than it was ever shown on maps—with the South Atlantic Ocean flowing along on the left. He looked farther north and east toward the great landmass of Asia and knew that as the world turned, he might even be able to make out the familiar shape of Australia.

But how could he ever get back down to it? he wondered. He had never floated so far off the ground before—there had always been someone to catch him, or something to hit his head on and stop him from drifting any farther up. But not this time. Now he was just an eight-year-old boy floating away from planet Earth into the darkness of the night sky and the mysteries of what lay beyond.

I'll never get home again, thought Barnaby, feeling the tears forming in his eyes. *And I'll never have any more adventures.*

And then, looking into the darkness, he thought he saw a small white dot in the distance, in the very direction in which he was floating. He blinked and yawned, for the atmosphere was so different up here that it was difficult to stay awake, and he wondered whether he was drifting toward a star, and if so, should he be worried. He had read somewhere that they were made of white fire; if he collided with one, then he would probably be burned to a crisp. But there was nothing he could do about it. He continued to float closer to the white dot, which then turned into two dots, one considerably larger than the other but connected by what looked like a long white rope.

He waved his arms, his eyelids growing heavier and heavier, his body desperate for sleep, and turned toward it just as the smaller white dot appeared to turn in his direction and wave back.

An astronaut! thought Barnaby sleepily. *A spaceship!*

His eyes could stay open no longer, and the last thing he remembered before he passed out was an enormous pair of arms wrapping themselves around him and pulling him through the atmosphere toward the safety of the ship ahead.

Chapter 21

Twenty Thousand Leagues Above the Earth

Barnaby woke when he fell to the floor, hitting his head on a rubber mat. He opened his eyes and looked around, his heart pounding a little faster when he realized that there were six space aliens staring at him.

"Why do you look so scared?" asked the first one, who looked exactly like a Japanese man, except that he wasn't a Japanese man, of course; he was a space alien.

"Because you've assumed human identities to put me at my ease," said Barnaby, scrambling backward in the spaceship's cabin. "And you're going to eat me."

"Eat him?" asked a rather elegant female space alien with a black bob, red lipstick, and a French accent. "Did he say eat him? I'm a vegetarian, for pity's sake."

"Who are you?" asked a third person, this time a young male space alien with a posh English accent.

"I'm Barnaby Brocket," said Barnaby.

"Well, I'm George Abercrombie," he replied. "And none of us are aliens, I'm happy to say. May I introduce Dominique Sauvet?" he added, nodding toward the Frenchwoman.

"Hello," she said.

"Naoki Takahashi," he continued, pointing at the first man, who quickly bowed from the waist before standing upright again.

"Over there is Matthias Kuznik," continued George, and a tall blond man stepped forward with a friendly smile on his face.

"Good to meet you," said Matthias, before turning to George a little apprehensively and shaking his head. "Should we be getting involved in this?" he asked. "We don't know who or what he is."

"Don't worry, Matthias, I'm sure he's perfectly safe. He's just a child."

"I'm *eight,*" snapped Barnaby, wounded to the core.

"And those two over there," said George, ignoring this interruption, "sitting in our recreation area, are Calvin Diggler—"

"Yo," said Calvin, nodding his head while munching on a pretzel.

"Calvin's from across the pond," said George apologetically. "You'll have to forgive his manners. The fact that he doesn't have any, I mean."

Barnaby looked around. "What pond?" he asked, frowning. "I don't see any pond."

"I don't mean a literal pond," said George. "*The* pond! The Atlantic Ocean. Calvin is one of our American cousins."

"Oh, I see," said Barnaby. "Are you all cousins, then?"

"No," said George, confused. "No, none of us are cousins."

"But you just said—"

"I didn't mean my literal cousin."

Barnaby stared at him, then turned to Matthias Kuznik with a questioning expression. "Why does he not mean anything he says?"

"He's English," explained Matthias.

"Yes, well, if I might just finish . . . ," continued George. "The last member of our crew is the little filly sitting next to Calvin."

"George!" snapped the woman, looking up from her book. "How many times have I asked you not to refer to me in equine terms?"

"Sorry, old girl," he said. "Don't get her riled, Barnaby, there's a good chap. That cat has claws."

"She's a filly *and* a cat?"

"I can be anything you want me to be, sugar," said the woman, whose name was Wilhelmina White, winking at him.

Barnaby blushed scarlet from his ears to his toes and didn't know where to look. When he managed to get ahold of himself again, however, he realized he'd recognized something familiar in her voice.

"You're not Australian, are you?" he asked, looking across at her.

"Close. I'm a Kiwi. Have you been there?"

"No, but I'm from Sydney," said Barnaby.

"You're a long way from Sydney up here," remarked George Abercrombie. "I have to say we were a little surprised to see you floating around out there. We don't get many visitors on *Zéla IV-19.*"

"What's *Zéla IV-19*?" asked Barnaby.

"Our spaceship," said Naoki Takahashi.

"Perhaps you could let us know what you were doing?" asked George. "Lashings of apologies, of course, for putting you on the spot like this, but let's be frank: it's a rum deal when an eight-year-old boy just rolls up out of nowhere and accuses a chap of being a space alien when a chap's clearly anything but."

Barnaby stared at him, blinked a few times, and looked around at the other crew members.

"Fourteen months," drawled Calvin Diggler from the rest area. "That's how long we've had to listen to that. You'd better get used to it, kid, if you're planning on sticking around."

"Steady on," said George. "A chap's just wondering what's going on, that's all."

"It's a long story," said Barnaby.

"Well, we're not going anywhere."

"All right, then," he said, starting at the very beginning—and over the next couple of hours, as they sat down to a meal of tomato soup served cold from stainless steel canisters, followed by five square tablets of food, each one a different color (one that tasted like roast chicken, another that tasted of mashed potatoes, a third of carrots, a fourth of mushy peas, and a fifth that was a delicious crème caramel), Barnaby told them the story of his life, from his early days in Sydney to the terrible thing that had happened at Mrs. Macquarie's Chair, and then the story of the last month and the extraordinary characters he'd met along the way.

"That's quite a tale," said Calvin. "Expect us to buy it, do you?"

"But it's the truth," insisted Barnaby.

"Then how come you're not floating in here?"

Barnaby thought about it. It was true. He hadn't floated since the moment he'd woken up in the spaceship. His feet were on the ground like everyone else's, and there was nothing in particular to hold him there.

"I don't know," he said, frowning. "I don't understand it. I promise that everywhere else I go, I float."

He stood up and wandered around the cabin, waiting for that particular feeling to come, but it never did. It was very strange to be able to just walk around like this without floating to the ceiling. Was this what it was like to be normal? It didn't feel normal. And it certainly didn't feel good.

"If anyone should be floating in here, it's us," said Naoki. "The air has to be depressurized and regulated; otherwise, we'd be hitting our heads on the ceiling."

"My parents would love to have that type of air back home," said Barnaby. "Do you think that's what's keeping me on the floor?"

"I doubt it," said Dominique. "If what you say is true, then you should still be floating. Unless it has something to do with the air compression. You ever get sore ears?"

"Yes, I do," admitted Barnaby. "When I'm made to stay on the ground against my will. They're never agonizing, but there's always a sort of throbbing pain."

"Ever had a doctor look at them?"

"My parents haven't taken me to a doctor since I was a baby," explained Barnaby. "They're embarrassed to let me out of the house."

Dominique considered this and nodded her head. "When you get back down to Earth," she said, "get your ears checked out."

"All right," said Barnaby. "But how much longer are we all going to be up here anyway? Are you going to live here forever?"

"No," said Dominique. "We're coming to the

end of our mission, and then we'll finally get to go home. We only have one more space walk to do—"

"My turn!" insisted Naoki, slamming his fist down on the table and making the tablets of food jump. "My turn!"

"All right, mate, we know it's your turn," said Wilhelmina. "Keep your wig on."

"Hmm," grunted Naoki, popping another carrot tablet in his mouth.

"My brother, Henry, wants to be an astronaut," said Barnaby. "He's obsessed with outer space."

"Well, this isn't outer space, I'm afraid," said George. "It's middle space. We're several hundred million light-years away from outer space. It's that way . . . ," he added, pointing a finger toward the left-hand side of the spaceship's rear before adjusting it ever so slightly. "No, actually, it's more like that way," he said, correcting himself.

"Have your parents sent him to Space Academy?" asked Calvin, and Barnaby shook his head.

"No, they want him to be a solicitor like them. They say normal people don't want to go to outer space."

"Middle space."

"*Any* part of space. They've told him that when he's eighteen, he should go to university to study law."

"I know how your brother feels," said Calvin, sniffing one of the crème caramel tablets, then deciding against it and throwing it back in the pile in the center of the table.

"Oh, but you've handled it!" cried George, looking aghast.

"Zip it, Prince Charles," snapped Calvin. "Trying to tell a story here. You should tell your brother that if he wants to be an astronaut, he needs to go to Space Academy. My parents refused to send me when I was a kid. Said I was too stupid."

"Too stupid?" asked George, still smarting from the way Calvin had spoken to him. "Oh, God forbid that anyone should think you're stupid. I bet you don't know the capital of Mozambique."

"Maputo," said Calvin without a moment's hesitation.

"Or what the square of the hypotenuse is equal to."

"The sum of the squares of the other two sides."

"Or where the Duke of Devonshire stands in succession to the throne."

"Fourteenth," said Calvin. "About a million and a half places ahead of you."

"Well," said George, sitting back irritably. "All right, so you're good on general knowledge. If I'm ever involved in a pub quiz, I'll drop you a telegram."

"If you ever drop me a telegram, I'll drop you on your head."

"All right, boys, that's enough," said Dominique in an exhausted tone. "Barnaby was telling us about his brother. And he's our guest. And, Calvin, we've heard how your parents didn't encourage you a hundred times before."

"I showed them, though." He pointed out through the porthole into the blackness beyond. "Space," he said, then pointed all around him. "Spaceship." Then he pointed at himself. "Astronaut."

"My parents wished for me to become professor of mathematics at Tokyo University," said Naoki Takahashi. "Like my mother and grandfather before me."

"You *are* a bloody good mathematician, Naoki," said Wilhelmina. "He knows all the numbers," she added, turning to Barnaby and nodding her head enthusiastically. "Even the really big ones."

"My parents thought there was something a little embarrassing about my desire to become an astronaut," said Dominique. "They wanted me to work in an art gallery and marry a writer who thinks the world doesn't appreciate him enough."

"Like there's any other sort," muttered Calvin Diggler.

"My parents don't talk to me anymore," said Matthias Kuznik, bowing his head in shame. "Back home in Germany I am a national disgrace."

"But you're an astronaut!" said Barnaby. "They should be proud of you."

"They *were* proud of me. Once," he said. "I was the greatest striker in the history of the German Football Federation. Better than Oliver Bierhoff. Better than Jürgen Klinsmann. Even better than the great Gerd Müller. By the time I turned twenty, I had already played for my country thirty times and scored sixty goals."

"Two in every match," said Naoki.

"I told you he was good with numbers," said Wilhelmina.

"Well, no," said Matthias. "Sometimes it was more, sometimes it was less, but on average, yes, it was two. Children looked up to me; they had my posters on their walls. But all the time I was playing football, I was training to be an astronaut too, and nobody knew."

"But then they should be twice as proud of you," said Barnaby. "You're a great athlete *and* an astronaut."

"You haven't heard the rest of it yet," said George.

"It was two weeks before the start of the World Cup," continued Matthias. "Everyone expected Germany to win as long as I played in every match. But just before the start of the tournament, I was contacted by the Space Academy to tell me that my number had been called and I had been selected for this yearlong mission. Only the mission began the following Tuesday. And the World Cup began on Wednesday night."

"Ah," said Barnaby.

"Exactly. I had to choose."

"And which did you choose?" asked Barnaby—the other six turning at that point to stare at him.

"Maybe he *is* an idiot after all," said Wilhelmina.

"No, no," said Barnaby, realizing his mistake. "Of course. You chose space. I get it."

"I chose space," agreed Matthias.

"And he's not much looking forward to going home, are you?" asked George.

"Not much," he admitted. "My family will want nothing to do with me."

"I was supposed to take over the family farm," said Wilhelmina, who didn't like to be left out of a good moaning session. "But I didn't want to spend my days shearing sheep and sending cattle off to market. My old man had to put one of my half-wit brothers in charge instead of me when I went to the academy. He hasn't spoken to me since."

"And what about you?" asked Barnaby of George Abercrombie. "Does no one in your family speak to you either?"

"I don't have a family," said George, looking down at the table and rubbing at an invisible stain there. "I wanted to be an astronaut because I was lonely. I only wish I had all these chaps' problems."

Which brought that particular conversation to an abrupt end.

Chapter 22

The Space Walk

Over the next few days, Barnaby got to know each of the astronauts a little better and grew to like them all. His favorite pastime on board *Zéla IV-19* was sitting on one of the cushioned seats by the portholes and staring down at the slowly rotating globe that was the planet Earth far below. In the morning he would look out and see North and South America and remember his time on both continents. And there was Canada at the top and the Atlantic Ocean, which, when he returned a few hours later and looked out again, led to Ireland. But the best time was at the end of the day, when he could make out Australia and New Zealand, those two familiar shapes that meant home. He was fascinated by the ring of green and blue that acted as a perimeter around the continent, and the browny-gray expanse in the center. He would stare at it for long periods of time, filling in the places like he used to do in geography class. Perth over here, a small dot on the west coast. Sydney over here on the southeast. Melbourne at the base, just above Tasmania. Uluru, north of center. Canberra, where the government worked, down in the south. Byron Bay, home of his favorite living writer. He'd come to their school once, and for weeks afterward the queues at the library doors stretched halfway down the corridor. In the evenings he swapped stories of antipodean life with Wilhelmina and was delighted to learn that when the spaceship finally returned to Earth in a few days' time, they would be touching down just outside Sydney.

"So I'll get to go home at last," said Barnaby.

"You sure will. Happy?"

Barnaby nodded, but for the first time, now that returning home seemed like an actual possibility, he started to feel a little uncertain. He wanted to go home, of course. He'd been trying to get back there for a long time, after all. So why did the prospect suddenly make him feel so nervous?

"Last space walk!" roared Naoki Takahashi on their final morning in space. "*My* space walk! Great pride for Naoki Takahashi! Great pride for Japan!"

"I'll get the suit," said Dominique, pressing a button on a wall. A hidden door opened to reveal a shiny white spacesuit.

"Wow," said Barnaby, his eyes opening wide as he stared at it.

"This is the most expensive thing on the spaceship," said Calvin. "Which is why there's only one of them. If we didn't have one of these, we wouldn't be able to breathe on our space walks."

"Or go where we want to go," added George. "It is made of a special material that allows us to control our movements out there. Otherwise, we'd just drift off through middle space and on into outer space."

"What do you do out there anyway?" asked Barnaby, who was intrigued by the equipment that was being brought up and the extraordinary white suit that Naoki was climbing into.

"We gather air samples," explained George. "Also the debris—flotsam and jetsam that floats through space. We measure air pressure and temperature. We take readings of sound and light as it travels to and from the Earth."

"Does this rope feel quite right to you?" asked Dominique of no one in particular. "The tension feels a little off somehow."

"We've all gone on space walks, Barnaby," explained Calvin, ignoring her. "Dozens of times. There's nothing to it. But it's vital information for the scientists and geologists back on the home planet."

"Can I go?" asked Barnaby, filled with enthusiasm now; this would be something to tell Henry when he eventually got home. "I'd love to go on a space walk."

“Sorry, kid,” said Calvin. “It’s not just for fun, you know. This is important scientific research. We can’t have any distractions.”

“Oh, please!” begged Barnaby, and for a moment he thought that the astronauts were going to allow it, but in the end they shook their heads.

Naoki Takahashi made his way through into a separate chamber, which was completely sealed before another door opened slowly on the opposite side and he stepped out into the vast unknown, his movements as graceful as a dancer’s. He stretched his arms wide, connected back to *Zéla IV-19* by nothing more than the strong white rope that Dominique had been uncertain about earlier.

“How long will he be out there for?” asked Barnaby, watching his every movement through the porthole, envying him this great adventure.

“Ninety minutes—we have to make sure to watch the clock,” said Wilhelmina. “He only has enough oxygen for that amount of time. If we leave him out there any longer, he’ll suffocate and die.”

It was difficult to make out exactly what Naoki was doing. Every so often he would remove some scientific instrument from one of his pockets, hold it out in front of him for a minute or so, then replace it in his pocket and zip it up. Sometimes he would take an unusually shaped bottle, open the lid, wait, reseal it, and zip that up too. It all seemed to be going perfectly.

Until something went wrong.

"The rope!" cried George, pressing his face against the porthole as the white cord that connected Naoki to the spaceship shivered and trembled for a few minutes, making the astronaut turn upside down and rotate. His arms flew out from his body, and he looked back at the spaceship with a confused expression on his face.

"I knew there was something wrong with it," said Dominique, panic rising in her voice. "I said as much. But everyone ignored me."

"Bring him back in," ordered George, and Matthias pressed the button that was supposed to wind the cord back into the spaceship and the astronaut back into the airtight chamber—but the moment he touched it, there was a horrible sound like elastic being pulled too far and breaking, or a balloon being inflated more than it should be and popping, and the white cord snapped, leaving Naoki Takahashi floating in space with no way to get back to them. He waved in their direction, and they waved back to indicate that they were working on the problem as they all gathered round the table with diagrams and schematics.

"We need to take a second cord out," said Calvin. "If we get him connected to the ship again, then we can reel him back in. I'll go out with one."

"No, I'll go," said George, who liked the idea of being a hero.

"If you're going to fight about it, then I'll go," said Dominique, who was already imagining her appearance at the Élysée Palace to accept her award for bravery.

"If anyone's going out there, it'll be me," insisted Wilhelmina.

"This is a tremendous joke," said Matthias, laughing heartily. "This clearly calls for German efficiency. It's a job that requires the attention of Matthias Kuznik."

"Talking about yourself in the third person again?" asked George, shaking his head. "That's exactly the kind of arrogance we don't need, thank you very much."

The astronauts all started to talk over each other, each insisting that they should be the one sent out to rescue Naoki. Barnaby glanced at the clock. The minutes were ticking away. So was Naoki's oxygen supply.

"I'll do it," he said in a quiet voice—so quiet in fact that the five astronauts didn't even hear him at first. "I said, I'll do it," he repeated, louder now, and they turned to look at him—a little irritably, as if he was just getting in the way.

"Don't be silly, Barnaby," said Wilhelmina. "You're not a trained astronaut. If we sent you out there, you'd lose control of yourself. You have to be used to floating."

"If there's one thing I am definitely used to,"

he said, rising up to his full height and placing his hands on his hips defiantly, "it's floating."

"Can we risk it?" asked Dominique, looking around. "He's just a kid."

"A kid who wants to help," said Barnaby. "And none of you can agree among yourselves. So please let me do it. It'll be an adventure. Plus, I'm brave, you know. Really I am. And time is running out."

They all looked out of the porthole toward Naoki, who was beginning to drift a little.

"Are you sure you can do it?" asked Calvin, putting his hands on the boy's shoulders and looking him directly in the eye.

"No," said Barnaby. "But I can give it a try."

"Good enough for me," said George. "All right, everyone. Let's get the rope. You take it out and give it to Naoki. He'll know how to reattach it to his suit. Once that's done, hold on to him and we'll reel you both in together—understand?"

"Got it," said Barnaby, trying not to think about the hundreds of butterflies floating around in his stomach.

And so he was fitted with a mask and a tank—great fun—and sent through the airtight chamber and out into space. It felt good to be floating again; he felt more like himself than he had since arriving at *Zéla IV-19* the previous week. It was peaceful out there too: all the noises and troubles of recent times seemed to fade away into nothingness. For a moment Barnaby thought how peaceful it would be to spend the rest of his life floating in space, never having to worry about anyone or anything except passing comets. But these pleasant thoughts were interrupted by the sight of Naoki Takahashi waving frantically at him and turning over and over in despair as he floated in all directions. Barnaby kicked his legs as if he was swimming and floated toward him, handing him the rope like he'd been told, and within a few seconds Naoki had reattached himself to the ship. Barnaby held on tight and the astronauts brought them both back inside.

"You're a hero, mate," said Wilhelmina later when they were all gathered for a celebratory meal of food tablets and purified water.

"Great shame for Naoki Takahashi," said Naoki sadly, bowing his head in despair. "Great shame for Japan."

"I like being an astronaut," said Barnaby, grinning. "Can I go for a space walk again?"

"Not now, sorry," said George, strapping himself into the front of the spaceship. "We can't risk any more disasters like that. There's only one place we can go now."

"Where's that?" asked Barnaby.

"Home."

LOST in SPACE

Chapter 23

Everything They've Told You Is True

The spaceship touched down near the Berowra Valley Bushland Park at three o'clock the following afternoon. On their descent, Barnaby started to feel that familiar floating sensation getting more and more pronounced, until he was forced to put on his safety belt or risk floating up to the capsule's ceiling.

Barnaby had never experienced anything like the noise that was produced when the front of the rocket detached itself from the rest of the capsule, leaving them flying along in something that looked more like a clunky aeroplane than anything else. Finally, the engines began to decelerate, the wheels descended, and they made it safely back to Earth. A long line of dignitaries from each of the countries that had provided an astronaut were on hand to welcome them back to the home planet. Science ministers from New Zealand, the United Kingdom, Japan, France, Germany, and the United

States jostled with each other to get to the front of the line in order to ensure that they would be in all the photographs, but the Australian foreign minister, who was used to dealing with unruly children, made them stand in a horseshoe shape and declared that only when each astronaut appeared could their government representative step forward. There was a lot of grumbling about this, but it *was* Australian territory, so Australian rules had to be obeyed. The British minister poked his French counterpart in the ribs and said, "It's all your fault, Luc," but the Japanese minister was having none of that sort of bullying and slipped behind him to give him a wedgie.

After the engines had been turned off completely, Justin Macquarie, a Sydneysider who not only was head of the International Space Academy but also happened to be a direct descendant of Lachlan and Elizabeth Macquarie, at whose chair in the Botanic Gardens a terrible thing had once happened, stepped forward and cleared his throat.

"Ladies and gentlemen," he said, tapping his finger against the microphone, "it gives me great pleasure to welcome *Zéla IV-19* back to Earth after a long and successful mission. These astronauts have brought great pride to each of their families—more perhaps than they might have done in any other field of human accomplishment. And now may I ask them to leave the spaceship and meet the welcoming committee, after which they should go directly through to baggage reclaim to collect their suitcases, which I believe are being delivered to carousel number four."

One by one the astronauts emerged, blinking, into the afternoon sunlight, a little unsteady on their feet as they descended the rocket's staircase. When all six were standing together in line, the band began playing the first of the six national anthems, and they were only in the middle of "La Marseillaise" when first the tuba player, then the saxophonist, then the violinist each stopped in surprise. The music became discordant and the conductor tapped his stand in embarrassment, but by now everyone's eyes had turned to the doors of the spaceship, where what looked like an eight-year-old boy had just emerged from *Zéla IV-19* with a parachute attached to his back.

"Who on earth are you?" asked Justin Macquarie, stepping forward.

"I'm Barnaby Brocket," said Barnaby.

"You speak our language!"

"Of course I do."

"How did you learn it?" asked Mr. Macquarie in a slow, careful voice, as if talking to a foreigner who had only a basic grasp of English.

"I don't know," said Barnaby, trying to remember when he had first learned to speak. "It's something I picked up when I was a baby."

"You assimilated it," said Mr. Macquarie, nodding thoughtfully. "From the conversation of the astronauts. You can learn, then. Perhaps we can learn from you too," he added loudly, a wide smile spreading across his face as he tried to look accommodating. "I'm sure there are many things that you can teach us."

Barnaby thought about it and shrugged his shoulders. "It's possible, I suppose," he said. "Although I haven't been to school for a while, so I might be a little rusty. My geography is pretty good, though. I'm quite well traveled for a boy my age."

The audience started to talk to each other in loud voices, but Justin Macquarie turned to hush them, afraid that their noise might antagonize the space creature. "You believe you are a boy?" he asked.

"Well, I *am* a boy," said Barnaby, confused. "I might be only eight, but I know the difference between boys and girls. And I am *definitely* a boy."

"How did he get in there?" shouted the German minister, looking around for a parent who might have allowed their child to slip under the barriers and run in to explore the spaceship.

"He's with us, sir," said Matthias Kuznik, but the German minister shook his head and turned away.

"I can't even look at you," he said quietly. "Fourth!" he added dramatically. "We couldn't even win the third-place play-off—the most pointless fixture in the global sporting calendar."

"Great shame for Matthias Kuznik," said Naoki Takahashi, shaking his head. "Great shame for Germany."

"But what do you mean, he's with you?" asked the New Zealand science minister.

"We found him," replied Wilhelmina White. "He just came floating toward us, so we took him in."

"Everyone inside," said Justin Macquarie, clapping his hands loudly at the microphone. "And put this boy in quarantine for the time being. I need to have a think about this."

At the word *quarantine*, two men dressed in yellow rubber protective suits with helmets covering their heads came running toward Barnaby, picked him up under each arm, and dragged him inside the terminal. They ran down some long corridors; up a flight of stairs; past a swimming pool, a sauna, and a decompression zone; then down again through a series of narrow passageways, where a code was punched into a keypad, and they entered a large white room to find a dozen white-suited scientists working together in perfect silence. The scientists turned in unison, stared at Barnaby, blinked, then returned to their test tubes and microscopes. In the corner of the room stood a glass cell with a single white seat inside.

"Code?" asked the scientist sitting closest to the glass cell, turning to one of the men holding Barnaby with an expressionless expression on his face, if such a thing is possible.

"Twenty—two—nine—twenty—nineteen—sixteen," replied the man. The scientist gave a barely perceptible nod of the head as he tapped the numbers into a computer, and the glass front opened silently. Barnaby was thrown inside, the doors closed, and he found himself alone, staring out at his captors. Of course, as he was no longer being held by the yellow-suited men, it was only a moment before he began to float upward and found himself pressed against the top of the glass box, looking out at them from above and counting their bald spots. One or two of the scientists glanced over and studied him for a moment, but they soon turned away; they had clearly seen many strange and unusual things in their lives—this would barely merit a place in the top one hundred.

"Help!" cried Barnaby, tapping on the glass. "Let me out of here."

"You're in quarantine," said one of the scientists, stifling a yawn.

"But why? I haven't done anything wrong."

"You're the space boy, aren't you? We can't allow space boys to just go wandering around Australia. Anything could happen. We have an environment to protect. If you'd been found smuggling peanut butter into the country, you'd be in the same predicament."

"But I'm not carrying any contamination!" protested Barnaby. "And I don't have any food on me! I don't even like peanut butter. It's all gloopy and sticks to your teeth."

"He's right, it does," said one of the scientists.

"You'll just have to wait for Mr. Macquarie to come," said another. "He'll know what to do with you."

"Mr. Macquarie knows best," cried all the other scientists in unison, turning to look at Barnaby, smiling for exactly four seconds, then turning back to their work. One put an enormous pair of headphones over his ears and placed a microphone on top of a piece of rock—one of the rocks that had been taken off *Zéla IV-19*—and listened. Nothing happened for a moment, then his eyes opened very wide and he seemed intrigued by whatever it was he heard.

"It's Schubert," he said, turning to one of his colleagues. "Listen, Celestine. It's Schubert, I'm sure it is."

"Rachmaninoff," said the lady sitting next to him, taking the headphones and shaking her head.

"No, I'm sure it's Schubert."

"You're wrong."

"The fact that it's anyone at all is the most interesting thing, surely," said the man sitting next to her, having a listen. He threw the headphones down and shook his head in disgust. "I hate rock music," he said, returning to his work.

Finally, the doors to the room opened and Mr. Macquarie reappeared, coming over toward Barnaby's glass box and looking up at him with a perplexed expression.

"I want to come in there and talk to you," he said. "If I step inside, you're not going to hurt me, are you?"

"Of course not," said Barnaby. "I wouldn't even know how."

"All right, then," said Mr. Macquarie, reaching over to the control panel. He tapped in the six numbers again and the doors slid open. "But just so you know, if you try anything funny, you'll only land yourself in a lot more trouble."

He stepped inside, sat down on the chair as the doors closed behind him, and looked up, shaking his head. "What are you doing up there anyway, Space Boy?"

"I'm not a space boy," insisted Barnaby. "How many times do I have to tell you? I'm from Kirribilli."

"I don't think we've tracked that planet yet," replied Mr. Macquarie. "Is it in our solar system?"

"Of course it is! It's right here in Sydney. Just down the road from the prime minister's house. You take the train to Milsons Point, go down the hill by the shops, turn left, and our house is down there."

"Are you quite certain?" asked Mr. Macquarie.

"Of course I am. I've lived there all my life."

"I have a sister who lives in Kirribilli."

"What's her name?"

"Jane Macquarie-Hamid."

"Oh, I know Mrs. Macquarie-Hamid," said Barnaby, a great smile spreading over his face. "She lives right across the road from us. My dog, Captain W. E. Johns, plays with her dog. They're the best of friends."

"If you know so much about her, then what's her dog's name?"

Barnaby thought about it. "Rothko," he said. "Rothko Macquarie-Hamid. Your sister puts a blue bow tie around his neck after she gives him a bath. Then Rothko comes straight across to ours so Captain W. E. Johns can pull it off with his teeth. No one should humiliate a dog like that, you know. You should mention it to your sister."

Mr. Macquarie seemed impressed that Barnaby knew the name of his sister's dog, and pulled a notebook out of his inside pocket, scribbled something down, then put it back. Barnaby hoped it was a note to his sister.

"Well, if you're not a space boy," he said finally, "then perhaps you wouldn't mind explaining to me just how you ended up inside *Zéla IV-19*. You must realize that if we send up six people to middle space, then we expect a maximum of six to return."

"Haven't the other astronauts told you?" asked Barnaby, thinking that if Mr. Macquarie didn't believe him, then he might at least believe *them.*

"They've told me a story, yes," he replied. "But it's so outlandish that I can't believe it."

"Everything they've told you is true," said Barnaby.

"But you don't know what they told me yet."

"Did they tell you that I floated up to their spaceship, fell asleep due to the air pressure, and was taken inside?"

"Yes."

"Did they tell you that I was born with a condition that means I don't obey the law of gravity and so can't stay on the ground for more than a few seconds at a time? When I was in the spaceship, I seemed to be able to do so, although I'm not quite sure why—it might have something to do with my ears?"

"They mentioned something about it," admitted Mr. Macquarie.

"Did they tell you that I saved Naoki Takahashi's life when the white cord snapped and he found himself floating around in outer space?"

"You weren't in outer space."

"Middle space, I mean."

"Yes, they told me all that. But look, Space Boy—"

"Stop calling me that! My name is Barnaby Brocket!"

"All right, then, Barnaby Brocket. But that's just the story of what you did up there. There doesn't seem to be any dispute about that. What I need to know is how you got up there in the first place."

And so Barnaby told him.

Every detail of his life story from the moment he was born to the moment when he asked the head of the International Space Academy to stop calling him Space Boy and to start calling him Barnaby Brocket instead.

"Well, I've heard some funny things in my time," said Mr. Macquarie when he was finished, "but that takes the biscuit. I suppose I don't have any choice but to believe you. The question is, what do we do with you now?"

"I could go home," suggested Barnaby.

"You could, that's true. But first things first. Before we let you go anywhere, we need to send you over to the hospital in Randwick to have a full checkup. Make sure you haven't come to any harm on your travels. Make sure you haven't picked up any space bugs."

Barnaby sighed. "All right, then," he said.

By the evening, Barnaby was lying in a hospital bed, a tight leather belt strapped across his middle to stop him from floating to the ceiling, waiting for the doctor to examine him. They had put him in a private room on the very top floor of the hospital. It was the best room they had, as there was an enormous skylight over the bed, about half the size of the room, and when he lay back, he could look up at the night sky above as it started to grow dark. Fortunately, the nurses had pressed a button on the wall next to him and sealed it, in case his belt came loose, to stop him from floating away. It felt strange to imagine that only a couple of days before, he had been out there in middle space looking down at the outlines of Australia and New Zealand in the distance; now he was lying in a bed in Sydney Children's Hospital staring up at the stars as they blinked in the darkness, wondering whether there were any other astronauts out there looking down at him.

A little while later, a doctor arrived, took a blood sample with a needle that simply punctured a tiny hole in the ball of Barnaby's thumb, then wrapped a large Velcro strip around his arm and kept pumping it tighter and tighter until it felt like it was going to squeeze his arm off altogether.

"Ow," said Barnaby Brocket.

"Oh, that doesn't hurt," said the doctor, whose name was Dr. Washington. She was quite a good-looking doctor, with dark black hair that she kept pushing behind her ears.

"No, it just felt tight, that's all," said Barnaby.

She smiled and tapped his knees with a rubber hammer to make sure they jumped, looked down his throat and into his eyes.

"Nothing wrong with you, so far as I can see," she said after a moment. "This whole floating business is a mystery, though, isn't it? When did it start?"

"About two or three seconds after I was born."

"That long? And you've been to see doctors about it?"

"When I was very small."

"And it's never gone away? You've always been like this?"

"Always," said Barnaby. "Every minute of my life." He sat back in his bed and then remembered something. "Except when I was in the spaceship," he said, and Dr. Washington, who was just about to leave the room, turned round and looked at him.

"What's that?" she asked.

"When I was in the spaceship, my feet stayed on the floor," he explained. "I floated to it and I floated out of it, but inside—"

"Where the air was pressurized—"

"That's what Dominique said! She told me to get my ears checked out when I got back to Earth."

Dr. Washington stared at him for a moment, then took a small instrument with a bulb at the end of it out of her pocket and looked inside his ears.

"Hmm," she said.

"What is it?" asked Barnaby.

"Just wait here a moment," said Dr. Washington—as if there was any chance of his being able to get up and leave. A few minutes later she returned with another doctor, Dr. Chancery, who took out of his pocket a black-and-silver contraption the size of a screwdriver that also had a bulb at the end; like Dr. Washington before him, he looked inside Barnaby's ears.

"Hmm," said Dr. Chancery.

"That's what I thought," said Dr. Washington. "Hmm."

"What is it?" asked Barnaby, starting to worry now. "What's wrong with me?"

"There's nothing wrong with you," said Dr. Washington. "Nothing wrong with you at all. You're a perfectly healthy little boy, in fact."

"So why were you looking inside my ears and saying 'Hmm'?"

"It's nothing for you to worry about," said Dr. Washington. "We'll just run a few tests, and then we'll have a better idea of what we're dealing with."

Barnaby said nothing, just stared up through the skylight and wished that sometimes, just once every century or so, a grown-up would give him a straight answer to a simple question.

A loud commotion from the corridor made him look up, and Drs. Washington and Chancery stepped outside to see what was going on. He could hear raised voices, then a scuffle, and then there was silence again. A moment later, Dr. Washington reappeared on her own, smoothing her hair down as if she'd just been in a fight.

"Sorry about that," she said.

"What's going on out there?"

"Reporters. From the tabloids. They've heard all about you, you see. How you can float. How you floated up to *Zéla IV-19.* They want to get your story for the weekend editions. I should probably tell you that they're offering you a lot of money for it. You're going to be famous if you're not careful."

Barnaby grimaced. That was the last thing he wanted. Famous people weren't normal, after all, and if he arrived in Kirribilli with a crowd of reporters in tow, then his parents would surely be even less happy to see him than ever. He might not even make it to see Captain W. E. Johns before he was dragged back off to Mrs. Macquarie's Chair.

"I don't want to speak to them," he said. "I just want to go home."

"I'm afraid we can't let you go until tomorrow afternoon at the earliest. We need to keep you in overnight to observe you. Plus, there are those tests I told you about—I won't have the results of them until lunchtime, and that might lead us in a different direction altogether. But if you like, I can call your parents and let them know that you're here and that you're safe."

Barnaby felt a slight burning sensation in his stomach at the idea of his parents arriving at the hospital while the press were still gathered outside. But he nodded and wrote his phone number down on a piece of paper, and Dr. Washington left him to get some sleep.

He stared up at the night sky once again, feeling his eyelids begin to grow heavy. Tomorrow he would finally see his parents again, not to mention Henry, Melanie, and Captain W. E. Johns, and be taken home to Kirribilli. But had anything really changed? He had been sent away from home because he was different from other boys, and although he might have learned a lot on his travels, he still hadn't learned how to keep his feet on the ground.

Chapter 24

Whatever Normal Means

The following morning Barnaby was sitting up in bed reading a copy of *Around the World in Eighty Days* that he'd borrowed from the hospital library. The sun was pouring through the skylight above him, shining directly down on the pages, illuminating Phileas Fogg's journey with his faithful valet Passepartout. He was thoroughly absorbed in the story—at the point where Phileas has missed the steamer from Hong Kong to Yokohama—when the door was flung open.

"Barnaby!" said two voices in unison, and he looked up to see two figures standing there, staring at him with slightly apprehensive expressions on their faces.

"Hello, Mum," he said, setting his book aside, surprised that he felt more anxious than happy to see them. "Hello, Dad."

"We wondered where you'd got to, son," said Alistair, coming over and attempting an awkward hug but changing his mind and shaking hands instead. Barnaby thought this was an extraordinary thing to say. He'd clearly been in on the plan, after all; he remembered their conversation over breakfast on his last morning at home.

"Hello, Barnaby," said Eleanor, leaning over and kissing him on the cheek, behaving as if nothing terrible had ever happened at Mrs. Macquarie's Chair. Barnaby breathed in her perfume; it had a familiar scent of home and made him lonely and sorrowful at the same time. "How are you feeling?"

"I'm fine," said Barnaby. "I'm not sick."

"Then you shouldn't be in hospital, should you? It's not normal to be in a place like this if there's nothing wrong with you."

"Try telling the doctors that," said Barnaby. "This is where they brought me. When I came back from space, I mean."

Eleanor sighed as she sat down on the corner of the bed, running a finger across the bedside locker and examining it for dust. "This whole space business is a lot of nonsense," she said. "And I'm tired of hearing about it already. It's not normal to want to go exploring worlds outside our own. We have a perfectly good planet right here, if you ask me."

"You're right there, Eleanor," agreed Alistair, sitting down on the only chair in the room. "I don't understand these explorers and what they think they're doing."

"But if there'd never been any explorers, then no one would ever have discovered America," said Barnaby.

"Well, exactly," said Alistair and Eleanor in unison, throwing each other a look.

After this they all remained silent for a few minutes as a great awkwardness descended on the room. Had they been able to see the paint on the wall grow infinitesimally fainter, then they would have seen it. Had they been able to hear the sound of their hair growing infinitesimally longer, then they would have heard it.

"How's Henry?" asked Barnaby, breaking the silence, wishing that his elder brother had come to see him in the hospital too.

"Henry's Henry," said Eleanor with a shrug, as if this was any sort of answer. "He's fine. Perfectly normal."

"And Melanie?"

"Also fine. Also perfectly normal."

Barnaby nodded, pleased to hear it. "What about Captain W. E. Johns?" he asked.

"Captain W. E. Johns has seemed a little sad of late, to be honest," said Alistair. "That tail of his has been on a bit of a go-slow."

"Nonsense," said Eleanor, contradicting him. "That's just the way dogs look. It's perfectly normal for a dog to look sad, and Captain W. E. Johns is a perfectly normal dog. On the inside he's chasing squirrels. Anyway, your brother and sister are going to come in and visit you in a little while. They're terribly excited about seeing you again."

"Can't I just come home?" asked Barnaby in a quiet voice, unsure whether they were going to say yes or no. "Can't I just see them there?"

"Of course you can," said Eleanor, sitting back a little, for the sun was pouring through the skylight above Barnaby's bed. "If that's what you want," she added in a quieter voice.

Barnaby thought about it. He assumed it was what he wanted. After all, where else would he go if not home?

"There's just one thing," said Alistair, coughing a little and sitting up straight as if he had some very important news to impart. "Your mother and I . . . well, we've discussed this ever since Dr. Washington phoned us last night to say that you were here. It has to do with this whole floating business of yours. Let's be honest, son: we've put up with it for as long as we can. Eight years, coming up to nine. Longer than most normal families would."

"We *are* a normal family, Alistair," insisted Eleanor, throwing him a filthy look before turning her attention back to Barnaby. "But your father's right. You've spent eight years floating up to the ceiling, lying around on your David Jones Bellissimo plush medium mattress, refusing to go to normal schools—"

"I didn't refuse to go anywhere," said Barnaby, sitting up in the bed. "*You* sent me to the Graveling Academy for Unwanted Children. I never wanted to go there in the first place."

"Oh, you're just splitting hairs now. The point is, if you're going to come home to Kirribilli, then you have to stop all this attention-seeking nonsense. First thing this morning the news vans were parked outside our house again, asking questions about the boy who came back from space, the boy who can't keep his feet on the ground, the boy who floats like a helium balloon. It's just like what happened when you insisted on being the ten millionth person to climb the Harbour Bridge."

"But I didn't even know that I was going to be the ten millionth person," cried Barnaby, feeling the injustice of it all now. "It was as much of a surprise to me as it was to you."

"You just have to draw attention to yourself, that's the problem. And we can't have that anymore. So we're asking you, Barnaby—if you come home with us, will you promise to be normal? Will you give up floating once and for all?"

"He might not have to promise, Mrs. Brocket," came a voice from the doorway, and they turned round to see Dr. Washington entering the room with a chart in her hands. She introduced herself to Barnaby's parents, gave him a quick once-over with a stethoscope and thermometer, then smiled at them all. "I think I might have some good news for you," she said.

"Well, we could all do with a little of that," said Eleanor in an exhausted tone. "What is it?"

"I wonder, did you ever bring Barnaby to see an ear specialist? When he was little, I mean?"

"No," said Eleanor, shaking her head. "The boy was on the ceiling most of the time. And there's nothing wrong with his ears. They're perfectly normal. But why do you ask?"

Dr. Washington hesitated for a moment and consulted her chart before nodding, apparently satisfied with her conclusions. "Yesterday," she explained, "when your son was brought in, I was asked by the Space Academy to give him a complete medical to make sure that he hadn't brought any space bugs back to Earth inside his body."

"You're not saying he has, surely?" cried Eleanor, throwing her arms in the air. "Is this to be his latest foolishness? Acting as a host for some malevolent intergalactic life-form?"

"No, he's perfectly fine, Mrs. Brocket," said Dr. Washington, shaking her head. "In fact, he doesn't seem to have had any adverse reaction to being in outer space for the last week at all."

"Actually, it was middle space," said Barnaby.

"Well, wherever it was, he seems to have survived

the ordeal perfectly well. Nor has he suffered any injuries from having circumnavigated the globe since you unluckily lost hold of him in Sydney," she added, raising an eyebrow as if she found this a little suspicious anyway.

Eleanor shifted uncomfortably in her chair and found something to stare at through the skylight.

"But what I did discover," continued Dr. Washington, "is an imbalance in Barnaby's ears. The alignment of the superior canal, the posterior canal, and the horizontal canal is completely out of kilter. The canals converge, you see, and control our sense of balance. That means that the air pressure inside his head is inconsistent, and no matter what he does, he's going to float. Actually, if you want to be absolutely scientific about this, he's not floating at all. He's falling."

"Falling?" asked Alistair and Eleanor, staring at her in surprise.

"That's right. In most people, the arrangement of the canals ensures that we obey the law of gravity, but in Barnaby's case, as all three are inverted—they're turned upside down—his brain can't interpret the signals it's being sent. It thinks that everything is the wrong way round. And so Barnaby finds himself falling up rather than down because his brain thinks that's the direction he should be headed. We insist on staying on the ground; he insists on rising away from it.

"It also explains why he didn't float in the spaceship," continued Dr. Washington. "The air is pressurized so that the astronauts don't float up and hit their heads on the ceiling. The same process aimed at Barnaby kept him on the ground, but the air up there is the opposite of what it is down here. Back on Earth, the astronauts won't float away. But Barnaby will. Does that make any sense?"

"Not much," said Alistair.

"It sounds completely abnormal," protested Eleanor.

"Well, it's not common, I'll give you that. But the thing is, it can be fixed."

Alistair and Eleanor sat up now and stared at her. "It can?" asked Eleanor.

"It most certainly can," said Dr. Washington. "I can do it myself, in fact. It's a very simple operation. It wouldn't take more than an hour or two."

"And when it's over?"

"When it's over, Barnaby won't float anymore. He'll be like everyone else. He'll be normal. Whatever normal means."

And at those three words, Dr. Washington smiled, Alistair grinned, and Eleanor looked as if she might be about to scream in delight and dance a little jig around the room. The only person who looked unsure about how to greet this potentially life-changing news was Barnaby himself, but then no one was looking at him or seemed at all interested in his opinion on the matter.

"How soon can you do it, doctor?" asked Alistair. "Would you like us to hold him down for you right now? I'm sure he wouldn't need an anesthetic. He's a very resilient little boy. Made of stern stuff."

"Perhaps not *right* now," replied Dr. Washington, making a note on her chart of something she wanted to discuss with the hospital psychiatrist later. "But today is certainly an option. I could fit Barnaby in for surgery around six o'clock if you wanted to go ahead with it. Then a night's rest here and some more observation over the next twenty-four hours, and Barnaby should be able to go home at some point tomorrow evening."

"And you're absolutely sure he'll be normal?" asked Eleanor.

"As normal as you or your husband anyway."

Which was good enough for Alistair and Eleanor Brocket.

Chapter 25

That Familiar Floating Feeling

Later that day, Henry and Melanie also visited the hospital. They were carrying a leather holdall, slightly unzipped at the top, whose contents seemed to be shaking and rattling. When Melanie laid eyes on her younger brother lying in the bed, she placed it on the floor and it seemed to curl up on itself and remained completely still.

"Barnaby!" she cried, rushing forward and throwing her arms around him. "We missed you so much. Every time I looked at the empty ceiling, I burst into tears."

"Hello, Barnaby," said Henry, giving him an affectionate hug. "How are you anyway?"

"I'm fine," he said. "I've had lots of exciting adventures. Met lots of unusual people. Seen lots of interesting places."

"Would you like to know what's been going on here in Sydney?" asked Melanie.

"Yes, of course!"

"Absolutely nothing," she said, pulling a face. "It's so boring here. Nothing ever happens."

"But it's the most magnificent city in the world!"

"Says you. I wish I could go off and have lots of adventures. You're so lucky."

Barnaby didn't know what to say to this. He wasn't accustomed to people envying him.

"What happened after I went?" he asked, for he was eager to know how his disappearance had been explained in the Brocket household. "What did Mum and Dad say? Did they talk about me a lot?"

"A little at first," said Melanie. "Then, when it seemed as if you weren't coming back, not so much. They said it was your fault that you'd floated away like that."

"I don't think it was *entirely* my fault," said Barnaby, a bit aggrieved.

"Well, no," said Henry. "Not entirely, I suppose. But you really should have done as you were told."

Barnaby frowned. "Did as I was told?" he asked. "How do you mean?"

"Well, Mum told us how you said it was too hot that morning to wear your rucksack," explained Melanie. "She said she'd told you that you had no choice, that you had to keep it on or you'd float away, but that you were in one of your moods and wouldn't listen to her."

"She told us that you took it off out of badness,"

said Henry. "And up you went. She tried to catch you but the wind picked up, and before she knew it, you'd risen too high."

"I think they've forgiven you, though," said Melanie.

"Of course they've forgiven him," said Henry. "Why, they're just happy to have you back safely. What's the matter, Barnaby? You've gone a funny color. That is what happened, isn't it?"

Barnaby opened his mouth, feeling a great ball of fury rising in the pit of his stomach. He'd been away from home for weeks; sometimes he'd barely eaten, sometimes he hadn't known where he was going to get a bed for the night; he'd been criticized on more than one occasion for smelling a little ripe. Sometimes he'd been really frightened and felt very alone. He looked at his brother and sister, wanting to tell them exactly what had happened and how he'd got himself into this situation in the first place, but their anxious expressions made it clear that not only did they believe their parents' version of events, but they needed to believe it too. Anything else, after all, was simply too awful to contemplate.

"Yes," he said finally, swallowing and turning away, unable to look them in the eye. "Yes, that's what happened. I should have listened to her. But you know me, I always have to have my own way."

"Well, that *is* normal," said Henry, smiling at him.

Before they could say any more, the door opened and a nurse—a rather bad-tempered nurse—looked inside and seemed appalled by what she discovered there.

"Children!" she said. "There can't be any children in here!"

"But it's a children's hospital," said Barnaby.

"*You* can stay," she snapped, pointing a finger at him. "But these two? Out! We don't allow children like you to come in here and spread your horrible infections to the patients. Out now! All of you! Except you," she added, pointing at Barnaby. "Out, out, out!"

Henry and Melanie sighed and turned back to their brother.

"We'll see you tomorrow, Barnaby," said Melanie. "After your operation."

"Mum told you about that, did she?"

"Yes, she's very excited."

"Out!" insisted the nurse, practically screaming now. "Out, out, out!"

"Oh, and we brought you a present," said Melanie quickly as she jumped off the bed, using the toe of her boot to push the leather holdall closer to him. It started to shake again, then settled a little, then shook again. Then settled again. "Don't open it now, though," she added, her eyes growing wide as if she was trying to impart a secret message, her head nodding in the direction of the nurse. "Wait until we're gone."

They made their way out into the corridor before they could be scolded any further, and the door closed behind them, leaving Barnaby alone in his room. He looked down at the bag, wondering what could possibly be inside, and as he unzipped it, to his great surprise, something leaped out and threw itself onto the bed in front of him.

"Captain W. E. Johns!" cried Barnaby in delight as the dog scrambled up the mattress and licked Barnaby's face so heartily that it was just about the best wash he'd had in weeks.

In the afternoon, a couple of hours before his operation was due to take place, a hospital porter brought a wheelchair and said that if he wanted to have a change of scenery for a little while, then he could wheel himself around the corridors. As Captain W. E. Johns hid under the bed, Barnaby jumped into the chair, buckled himself in, and set off to explore.

Everywhere he looked, there were children wearing pajamas and dressing gowns, either walking up and down the corridors with their parents or lying in the wards as their families gathered around, playing games of chess, backgammon, or Scrabble, or simply catching up on their reading. As far as he could make out, he was the only person who had been left on his own.

Turning a corner, he saw Dr. Washington sitting at a desk, tapping information into a computer and scribbling notes on a pad as she copied information off the screen, and wheeled himself over toward her.

"Hello, doctor," he said.

"Hello, Barnaby," she said, turning to look at him with a smile. "And what can I do for you?"

"I just wanted to ask . . . ," he began, thinking about this question carefully. "What would happen if I don't have the operation?"

"Well, you have to have the operation," she said, as if there was simply no question about it. "Your parents have already signed the forms, and I'm afraid when it comes to eight-year-old boys, they get to have the final say."

"Yes, but in theory," said Barnaby. "If they hadn't signed the forms, I mean. If they didn't want me to have the operation."

"But they do."

"But if they didn't."

Dr. Washington thought about it for a moment and shrugged her shoulders. "Well, nothing would happen as such," she said. "You'd remain exactly as you are. You'd keep floating. You'd never be able to keep your feet on the ground."

"And I'd stay like that forever?"

"Well, yes, I suppose so," said Dr. Washington. "But you don't have to worry, Barnaby, that's not going to happen. We're going to fix you up. By this time tomorrow you'll be a completely different boy. Everything in your life will have changed, and you'll be just like everybody else. Isn't that wonderful?"

Barnaby smiled, said that he was sure it was, then wheeled himself back to his room, back to his thoughts, back to Captain W. E. Johns.

It was getting late now. Almost five-thirty. The operation was set for six o'clock. Barnaby knew that the hospital porter would come for him at any minute; he'd be strapped onto a gurney and rolled down the corridor, pushed into a lift, and taken down into the depths of the building, where he would be sent to sleep. When he woke up again, he would be someone else entirely. He'd still be Barnaby Brocket, of course, just a very different Barnaby Brocket from the one who'd existed for the previous eight years.

He stared up through the skylight at the pale blue evening sky, at the wispy clouds that were floating by, at the birds making their way to wherever birds make their way to, and patted Captain W. E. Johns, who was lying curled up in a ball on his lap. And he thought about everything that had happened to him since the day Eleanor had cut a hole in his rucksack and let the sand run out.

He'd been in a hot-air balloon. He'd met two wonderful old ladies who'd never looked back after being thrown out by their families for being different. He'd visited a coffee farm in Brazil and got to cuddle up to a girl called Palmira. He'd had his rucksack stolen in New York and helped a young artist become successful. He'd taken a train ride to Toronto, seen a football game, floated up a tower, where he'd been saved and then kidnapped by a horrible man—but on the plus side he'd come across the most unusual and nicest people he'd ever met in his life. He'd even seen his friend Liam McGonagall again. He'd taken a bungee jump (or tried to) and a parachute jump (or tried to) and met a man who'd agreed to return to his children, even though they wanted to control everything he did with his life.

He'd even been to outer space.

Or middle space anyway.

And now he was back here again. Back in Sydney. Back in the normal world.

And it occurred to Barnaby that being normal might not be everything that it was cracked up to be. After all, how many so-called normal boys had had the adventures he'd had or met the people he'd met? How many of them had seen so much of the world and helped so many people along the way?

And who was to say that he was the one who wasn't normal anyway? Was it normal to cut a hole in a rucksack and send an eight-year-old boy off to who knew where? Was it even normal to want to be so, well, *normal* all the time?

From outside in the corridor he heard the sound of the lift doors opening and a trolley being pushed into the corridor. *That must be for me,* he thought, his heart starting to beat a little faster inside his chest. *If I let them take me away, they'll turn me into them.*

Which was when he realized that he *liked* being different. It was the way he'd been born, after all. It was who he was supposed to be. He couldn't allow them to change that. He didn't want to spend his whole life feeling like he had the afternoon he'd climbed the Sydney Harbour Bridge.

He looked up at the skylight above him, and then at the button that sat next to his bed—the one controlling the mechanism that opened and closed the window.

He looked at it.

He hesitated.

And then he pressed it.

New adventures, he thought. *New places. New people.*

People who won't cut a hole in my rucksack.

With a click and a sweeping sound, the skylight

started to open, and Captain W. E. Johns stirred in his lap, opened his eyes, and looked up at his master, offering him an enormous yawn.

"I'm sorry, boy," said Barnaby. "I can't let them change me."

Captain W. E. Johns stared at his master with a puzzled expression on his face. Barnaby looked up toward the skylight, which had opened fully now, allowing a cool breeze to drift into the room, and started to unbuckle the strap that was keeping him tied to the bed.

The dog stumbled to his four feet and tried to find his footing on the blanket. The expression on his face suggested that he wasn't sure what was happening but he was predisposed to disapprove of it. "Bark," he barked, just to be on the safe side.

"Shh," said Barnaby, that familiar floating feeling taking him over as the straps began to loosen—that wonderful sensation, that phenomenon that made Barnaby Brocket the boy he was.

Captain W. E. Johns began to panic now, his tail twirling in confusion, turning clockwise at first, then counterclockwise, then rotating back and forth in bewilderment. He tried to fasten the belt again with his teeth, but without success; there was no way it was possible for a dog.

"I'm sorry," said Barnaby, starting to rise now, his legs appearing from under the covers, his feet slipping out into the cold air. "I'll never forget you. I promise."

The dog barked once more, but it was too late. Barnaby was already out of the bed and starting to rise toward the ceiling. But before he could reach the skylight, the dog gave one last leap and wrapped himself around the boy's legs. They hovered in the air for a moment, the weight settling, but he was not a fat dog, and within a few seconds they started to rise again.

"What are you doing?" shouted Barnaby. "Get down! You can't come with me!"

But Captain W. E. Johns had lost his master once before; there was no way he was going to lose him again.

Barnaby felt a surge of panic; a part of him wanted to kick his feet back and forth until the dog had no choice but to let go and fall back onto the hospital bed. Another part of him, however, the stronger part, didn't want to move a fraction.

"All right, then," he said finally as they slipped through the skylight and into the outside world. "But you'd better hold on tight!"

into the night

Chapter 26

The Most Magnificent City in the World

The sky at night is a magical place.

There are so many things moving to and fro, leaving here, going there, that the human eye can barely discern the movement and the civilizations that are changing the universe in extraordinary ways, offering a burst of starlight over one city, an outbreak of thunder over another, a flash of lightning over a third.

But anyone staring into the sky over Sydney on that particular night, anyone who was prepared to open their eyes and see not just the darkness of the night or the whiteness of the moon, would have seen something extraordinary, something that—if they were willing to look—might have taken their breath away and made them realize that not everything in the world is open to a simple explanation.

On that night, looking out over the Kirribilli shoreline, they would have seen a police helicopter shining its bright searchlight across the bridge, the wonderful Sydney Harbour Bridge, with its steely crossbeams and proud flags waving in the night air, assisting the cars that drove to and fro—for a light on the bridge had blown out earlier that evening and no one wanted an accident.

They would have seen a star flickering and flashing on and off for a few minutes before disappearing entirely as it vanished forever, almost twenty million years after it had first blinked its way into existence—just a blaze of light at first, then a mass of fire, then a glowing burst of luminosity, then nothing, just a memory, just a hint of what had once provided a sparkle in the darkness.

And they would also have seen—if they had looked very closely—an eight-year-old boy rising through the clouds, a small loyal dog of indeterminate breed and parentage holding tightly on to his legs, disappearing into the darkness of a fine Australian night, heading who knew where, uncertain when his feet would touch the ground again.

A boy who was ready to meet new people.

A boy who wanted to have new adventures.

And above all else, a boy who was proud to be different.